JOY FOR BEGINNERS

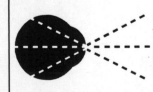

This Large Print Book carries the
Seal of Approval of N.A.V.H.

JOY FOR BEGINNERS

ERICA BAUERMEISTER

WHEELER PUBLISHING
A part of Gale, Cengage Learning

GALE
CENGAGE Learning

Detroit • New York • San Francisco • New Haven, Conn • Waterville, Maine • London

GALE
CENGAGE Learning™

LIBRARY OF CONGRESS CATALOGING-IN-PUBLICATION DATA

Bauermeister, Erica.
  Joy for beginners / by Erica Bauermeister.
    p. cm.
  ISBN-13: 978-1-4104-4074-7 (hardcover)
  ISBN-10: 1-4104-4074-5 (hardcover)
    1. Female friendship—Fiction. 2. Self-actualization (Psychology) in women—Fiction. 3. Large type books. I. Title.
  PS3602.A9357Y43 2011b
  813'.6—dc22   2011022694

Published in 2011 by arrangement with G. P. Putnam's Sons, a member of Penguin Group (USA) Inc.

Printed in the United States of America
1 2 3 4 5 6 7 15 14 13 12 11

For Gloria and Marjorie

Tell me, what is it you plan to do with your one wild and precious life?

— *Mary Oliver*

PROLOGUE

Life came back slowly, Kate realized. It didn't come flooding in with the reassurance that all was well. The light outside was no different; her daughter's body, the strength of her hug, was not necessarily more substantial. The delicate veil Kate had placed between herself and the world was not flung away. It clung.

But life is persistent, slipping into your consciousness sideways, catching you with a fleeting moment of color, the unexpected and comforting smell of a neighbor's dinner cooking as you walk on a winter evening, the feeling of warm water running between your fingers as you wash the dishes at night. There is nothing so seductive as reality.

The women were due to arrive soon; it was quiet in the house, and Kate was glad of the impending company. She was still not used to being alone with her body. For the past eighteen months it had been the property of

9

others — doctors certainly, but also friends, relatives, her daughter — its boundaries and capacities something they measured, gambled on, watched with loving or terrified or clinical eyes. Now the medical professionals had declared it hers again, handing it back like an overdue and slightly scuffed library book. In the weeks between the doctor's appointment and her daughter's departure for college, Kate had filled the space around them with lists and plans, shopping trips for desk lamps and extra-long twin sheets for Robin's freshman dorm room. Now Robin was off and away and Kate felt sometimes as if she was living in two empty houses, one inside the other.

So it was nice to have the prospect of guests, even if they were hell-bent on jubilation. Kate had heard the excitement in her friends' voices when she invited them to dinner, a thank-you for all they had done for her, she explained. But Marion had quickly renamed the evening a victory party and insisted that it be a potluck.

"You wouldn't take the fun out of it for us, would you?" Marion had asked.

As Kate moved about the kitchen from stove to refrigerator to sink, she passed the bulletin board that served as a central hub for reminders and memories, its surface a collage of photographs, a calendar, old ticket stubs and coupons and take-out menus. The week before Robin had left for college, she had surreptitiously added a brochure. Kate had spotted it in the morning when she came into the kitchen to make coffee — the glossy photograph leaping out at her, an extravagantly yellow raft vaulting through churning brown waves, water drops flying off its sides in rainbows. Kate's friend Hadley, who had once worked in marketing, always called those photos "adventure porn."

When Robin had come through the kitchen, Kate pointed to the brochure with a raised eyebrow.

"They've got two openings for next summer," Robin said. "Wouldn't it be fantastic?"

Kate had looked at her daughter's eyes, so full of anticipation and, deep underneath, a plea for normalcy. They had spent too much of the past year in a world full of exit doors, Kate thought. They could both use a promise that they would be here a year from now.

How could you say no? And yet as Kate had looked at the raft, the water, the size of it all, that had been exactly what — in fact the only thing — she wanted to say.

The doorbell rang, ten minutes early. Caroline, guessed Kate with an inward smile, as she opened the door.

"I thought you might want some help," Caroline said as she entered, arms overflowing with a wooden salad bowl and a bottle of champagne. She put them down on the small table by the front door and gave Kate a quick, fierce hug.

"What needs doing?" she asked, as she headed toward the kitchen.

Kate followed her and gestured to the wrought iron table on the back patio. Caroline walked over to the silverware drawer, sidestepping around Kate, who had opened the refrigerator to get out the sour cream.

"Cloth napkins?" Caroline asked, a fistful of forks in her right hand.

"The green ones in the sideboard."

"How's the house without Robin?" Caroline called as she rummaged through the drawer in the dining room, pulling out seven napkins.

"Quiet. And yours?"

"Empty." Caroline laughed softly. "We're quite the pair, aren't we?"

The kitchen was quiet for a few minutes. Kate could hear the soft clink of forks against knives as Caroline set the table outside. Kate lifted the foil on the pan and the scent of melting cheese and roasted

12

chicken, caramelized onions and a subtle undercurrent of salsa verde rose up from the pan. She inhaled memories.

The doorbell rang again.

"I'll get it." Caroline went through the house to the front door. "Marion's here," she called out.

"With the last tomatoes from my garden," Marion said, standing in the doorway, her hair loose and silver. "Hello, darling Kate." Marion took Kate in her arms and held her for a long moment.

Behind Marion came two younger women, one of them with a cake in her hands.

"Sara, did you bake that?" Kate asked, surprise in her voice.

"I wish — the only thing I've put in an oven since the twins were born is chicken fingers," Sara replied, pushing her hair back from her face with her free hand.

"She wouldn't have even made it out the front door if we hadn't been carpooling," Hadley commented and handed Caroline a loaf of bread.

"Last but not least," a voice came from the bottom of the stairs. "I'm no cook," Daria said as she entered, all red hair and curls, handing a bottle to Kate, "but I know a good wine when I see one. Now, can we start celebrating?"

■ ■ ■ ■

The plates were almost empty, the light gone early from the September sky. The edges of Kate's patio were lost in the foliage beyond, its contours lit by the back porch light and the candles on the wrought iron table, around which the women sat, talking with the ease of those who have settled into one another's lives. Out on the road the occasional car drove by, the sound muffled by the laurel hedge that held the garden within its green walls. Everything felt softened, the garden more smells than sights, emitting the last scents of summer into the air.

Kate looked at the women around her. It was an incongruous group — it reminded Kate of a collection of beach rocks gathered over time by an unseen hand, the choices only making sense when they were finally all together. Daria and Marion were sisters, Sara and Hadley neighbors; Kate and Caroline had met when their children were in preschool — individual lives blending and moving apart, running parallel or intersecting for longer or shorter periods of time due to proximity or a natural affinity. It had taken the birth of Sara's twins, and then Kate's illness, to weave their dissimilar con-

14

nections into a whole.

Kate heard a voice coming through the house.

"*There* you are . . ." A woman, dressed in a loose-fitting jacket and slim jeans, came out onto the back porch. "I'm sorry I'm late; my flight was delayed." She ran down the steps to the patio and hugged Kate.

"Ava," Kate said, holding her.

"Did I smell my mother's enchiladas?" Ava asked, and Kate smiled.

"I saved you some." She started for the kitchen.

"No, you don't," Caroline quickly interjected. "You're the queen tonight. You shouldn't have to wait on anybody." She sent a pointed look in Ava's direction.

"I'll get more wine," Daria added, following Caroline into the house.

Kate pulled a chair up next to her and motioned for Ava to sit down.

Now they were all here, Kate thought.

Daria came out the back door, the glossy brochure in one hand. "Hey, what's this?" she asked. "I found it tacked to the bulletin board."

"Robin wants the two of us to go rafting down the Grand Canyon," Kate said.

"But . . . ?" Caroline had come out on the

15

porch and was watching Kate's face.

"Have you seen those rapids?" Kate replied.

The women around the table nodded in understanding, although if they were to be honest none of them had ever experienced the Grand Canyon other than to stand on its rim and look down to the river below, which looked only green and far away from that distance. But that, of course, didn't matter. The women ranged in age, but they were all old enough to know that in the currency of friendship, empathy is more valuable than accuracy.

"It's scary," Caroline agreed, coming down the steps and setting a plate in front of Ava.

"Which is *exactly* why she should do it," Daria broke in. "Kate, you're here; you're alive. You should do something crazy to celebrate."

Kate simply shook her head and sipped from her wineglass, her thoughts traveling far from them, underwater. It was dark there, cold, where the waves grabbed you and took your life where you didn't expect it to go.

"Maybe we should give her some space," Sara suggested.

The women shifted in their seats. Ava

picked up her fork and took a bite of enchilada, closing her eyes in happiness. Kate smiled, watching her.

"All right," Marion said, leaning forward. "Here's a thought. Kate, when is the trip?"

"Next August." Kate regarded Marion suspiciously.

"Well, then," Marion continued calmly. "I propose we make a pact. If Kate agrees to go down the Grand Canyon, we'll each promise to do one thing in the next year that is scary or difficult or that we've always said we were going to do but haven't." She scanned the circle. "Everybody in?"

The women looked about at each other. One by one, they nodded in agreement.

Marion turned to Kate.

"All right?" she asked.

It was still for a moment. On the other side of the hedge, a car door opened with an electronic beep; the jingle of a dog's collar passed by.

"All right," Kate replied finally — and then she smiled. "But here's the deal. I didn't get to choose mine, so I get to choose yours."

CAROLINE

Things held on to Caroline — the ends of her sleeves caught by doorknobs, her coat in a car door, the knit of her Irish sweater snagged on an errant nail that no one had ever remembered seeing sticking out of the wall. But she had never been as good at catching, holding on to things — taxicabs, elevator doors, a husband, slipping closed and past, already on their way to another floor, another life.

Her son had nestled into her heart, all tousled hair and awkward elbows, and then he was off to college. Her parents had died. And now Jack had left her, rocketing like a boy down a water slide into the exuberance of his new, defiantly not-middle-aged existence.

"I should learn to be slippery," Caroline said to Marion when they met for coffee a few days after Kate's celebration in the garden. "I need to be sleek and unobtain-

18

able. All silk suits and no commitments."

"You know what silk is made out of," Marion commented mildly. She pushed her silver hair back from her face and studied her friend.

Marion was a person who had held on to Caroline. They had met years before, when Marion was writing an article about public yet intimate gathering spots, the modern equivalents of the old woodstove in the general store of pioneer days. The bookstore where Caroline worked was a perfect example, designed as a place to linger as much as shop — incorporating a bakery and cafe, a fireplace surrounded by oversized chairs for colder days and a patio outside for summer ones. It could have felt chaotic, a party full of strangers unable to introduce themselves, but instead was more like a genial conversation — the metallic clink of silverware set against the contented sigh of a book being slid from its shelf, the murmured comments of a knitting group seated at a round table in the three-sided alcove that held — was it intentional or simply serendipitous? — the house/garden/cooking books. Smells of cinnamon and yeast settling in between the covers of books only to rise from the pages when they were opened later at home.

Caroline loved the store. She had started going there almost twenty years before, when her son was in preschool and they would go for story hour. Caroline would buy a mug of coffee and watch her little boy, engrossed, listening to tales of muddy dogs and brave princesses. A few years later, when Brad was in elementary school and she was in what she would later call her "writing phase," she had come to the bookstore in the mornings to sit at one of the wooden tables in the cafe, pretending to write but really just allowing her eyes to slow and settle on the collage of mismatched chairs around her, the wide-plank pine floors, the way the bookshelves created a child-sized maze behind her. The espresso machine would make its hissing noise and she would listen to the conversations around her, to lives that were more or less interesting than her own. Later in the evening at home, Jack would ask her what she had written, or rather, how much. She would lie and tell him the stories she had heard as if they were of her creation, grateful for the loan of them, for the free pass they gave her into a few hours floating in a world not of her own making.

After a while, however, it became obvious

that the stories were not connected, were not in any case going to be a book, and Caroline had been grateful once again for the bookstore and the job she was offered as its used-book buyer. Brad had been well ensconced in school by that time, and Caroline had loved dropping him off and driving to the bookstore, anticipating the smell of old paper and warm blueberry muffins, ground espresso beans and nutmeg and ink.

It was quiet behind the counter where people dropped off their bags and boxes of books, then went to wander among the shelves or drink coffee while she assessed the value of their reading habits. First, you had to get rid of the esoteric tomes no one else would want; the beach reads that everyone else had already read and sold, sand filtering out of their pages like used-up words; the books that had been stuffed into the bottom of backpacks along with, she was sure, old bananas. For books in good condition, she would offer a quarter of the original price in store credit. Less, if people wanted a quick exit and cash.

At first Caroline had seen the job of used-book buyer as a stepping-stone to the more exciting world of the new releases displayed at the front of the store, their words freshly printed, their meanings clean as new sheets.

But she quickly realized she had an affinity for the older books and their muted scents of past dinners and foreign countries, the tea and chocolate stains coloring the phrases. You could never be certain what you would find in a book that had spent time with someone else. As Caroline had riffled through the pages looking for defects, she had discovered an entrance ticket to Giverny, a receipt for thirteen bottles of champagne, a to-do list that included, along with groceries and dry cleaning, the simple reminder: "buy a gun." Bits of life tucked like stowaways in between the chapters. Sometimes she couldn't decide which story she was most drawn to.

After Jack left, Caroline had found herself standing at her counter, considering the boxes and bags of books in front of her. She was, she realized one day, being traded in for a new release — and as a used-book buyer she couldn't decide if it was the irony or the triteness of the analogy that she resented most.

The evening of Kate's victory party, Caroline had been afraid that Kate would challenge her to climb a mountain or go out on a date. But Kate's assignments were as quiet and unexpected as Kate herself. She had taken a handful of beach rocks from a huge glass bowl in the center of the table and handed one to each of them — as reminders, she said. Caroline was first, and Kate had reached across the table, putting the smooth oval into Caroline's hand.

"Your task is to get rid of Jack's books," she said, and Caroline had realized she would have preferred the mountain.

"I don't know if I can do it," Caroline said to Marion, lifting up her coffee cup. She saw the expression on Marion's face. "It's not just because they're Jack's," she explained. "They're books. It's not their fault — they didn't do anything to anybody; they deserve a home."

"So do you," Marion replied.

Caroline couldn't imagine a home without Jack, even though in reality she'd been living alone for nine months already. Jack had a new sleek condo downtown, bought before he even told her he was leaving, his signature on the purchase documents a commitment, he had explained. He'd bought it with his own money — his inheritance from his father. She remembered the money; Jack had said he wanted to hold it aside, for flying lessons. She had thought he meant it literally.

Now, with Jack and Brad both gone, walking through her house was like driving the curves of a familiar but poorly maintained country road. She leaned into its rhythms naturally as she walked in the front door, left her keys in the dish they had bought on a family trip to Hawaii, passed the couch she and Jack had rolled off one night when the bed was too far away, went into the kitchen where it still seemed more natural for Brad to be standing as a four-year-old, head barely at the height of the counter, asking her what was for dinner. Without thinking, she was the person that the house, the furniture, the ingrained patterns of family life expected her to be. And then when she least anticipated it there was a hole that had to be swerved around — Jack's favorite painting gone from above the fireplace, Brad's room cleaner than it ever had been before he went to college. How big would the holes in her life be if Jack's books were gone?

As a child, Caroline had always loved the feeling of being surrounded by books; she had spent summers in the library, winters under the covers of her bed, knees tucked to provide a prop for the book of her choice.

24

As she grew older, she had loved the idea of filling the shelves of her life with the roles of daughter, friend, girlfriend, wife, mother — like favorite novels she could take out anytime and reread. There was something satisfying in knowing that wherever she went, whatever she was doing, they were always a part of her.

Jack saw it differently. There was nothing romantic, apparently, in a well-stocked bookshelf.

"I'm just thinking," Marion noted, taking a sip of her coffee, "that it might be nice to figure out how *you* want to live."

"If you're going to tell me that I can make lemonade out of lemons, I'm going to hurt you."

"No, but I am saying you can make space for a life."

Marion was the oldest of their group, at the tipping point of fifty-five, although she didn't seem to worry much about it. She was one of those people everyone referred to as grounded — a term that, before Caroline met Marion, Caroline had always thought of in the electrical sense, a live wire somehow muted, made functional, its power dispersed and controlled. But with Marion, the word took on a new meaning. Marion was originally from the Midwest, a geographical inheritance that didn't so much cling as grow up through her. Her face had the openness of cornfields and river bottoms, a calm belief in herself nourished by thick, green summer air, the feel of slow water moving beneath the hull of a canoe. She had developed a love of gardening early in her life and she used her hands easily and naturally, whether it was touching the earth or the shoulder of a friend.

Marion and Caroline had often laughed at the differences between them — Marion relishing heat and time spent in the dirt, her close-cropped, getting-down-to-business fingernails often carrying thin, black crescent moons that even the most determined scrubbing couldn't seem to clean. Caroline, on the other hand, was at best a spade girl, her favorite plants held in small clay pots. Better yet, no dirt at all. Jack had always said Caroline's favorite garden was the ocean.

After her coffee date with Marion, Caroline went to the pool. There was no reason to hurry home and the thought made her pause in the changing room, one strap of her bathing suit in her hand, halfway up to her shoulder, looking at herself in the mirror. Everyone commented these days on how well Caroline had stayed in shape — a two-handed compliment, Caroline always thought, an acknowledgment of her forty-eight years held lightly in one palm. Good for you, people would say, applauding the effort, the action. Caroline had been an English major in college; she knew a verb when she heard one.

It would be decades before anyone would think to compliment Jack's new girlfriend that way. Caroline had seen her once at the local farmer's market, standing by the tomatoes, all round curves and glossy surfaces. Caroline had watched the young woman laughing effortlessly with the vendor, and told herself that tomatoes would soon be out of season, hard and tasteless as plastic — but the argument lay in her imagination, dull and powerless against the fecundity in front of her.

Standing in the changing room at the pool, Caroline remembered how when she was younger, people used to say she was beautiful — an adjective, and one that always made her a bit embarrassed. Back in those days, Caroline had felt more comfortable thinking of beauty as something separate from her, like a scarf or a coat you could check before going in to a show. She wondered now, however, if she had treated more things as a part of herself rather than an accessory, perhaps everything would have turned out differently. How long had she and Jack thought of themselves as in a marriage — a contract, a partnership — rather than married, entwined? Maybe adjectives like beautiful and married, the way they sent the tendrils of their meanings into your self and soul, were harder to trade in than nouns — coat, marriage, wife.

Or maybe the problem was that she spent her time thinking about adjectives and verbs while other people stood around looking like fresh-picked produce, Caroline thought as she grabbed her towel and headed out to the pool.

When Caroline got home that night, she sat on the couch in her living room, staring at the wall of books. Jack's books to the left of the fireplace, hers on the right. Caroline favored an alphabetical approach to shelving her books; she said it made it easier for other people to find them, which it did, but in reality she loved the process of finding a book through a rational process, only to open the pages and be caught in the memories of the person she had been when she first read it. And while Jack enjoyed reading, he hadn't cared as much about the organization of the books, his shelf in the living room more a central gathering place than a sorting system.

Caroline had always seen the differences in their approaches as a sign of their individuality, had even joked about it with friends when she gave informal tours of their house. Oh, that Jack. Oh, that Caroline.

Now Caroline stood, looking at the two walls of books, and wondered if perhaps she had misinterpreted the symbolism. She went over to Jack's side and took out the first book from the bottom shelf. Then she put it back.

Caroline's other responsibility at the bookstore was as hostess to the authors who came to sign books and read aloud to the groups that gathered in the soft, cushioned couches around the fireplace, the hard-back chairs arranged in rows. Caroline's job was to supply authors with proper directions to the store, to ascertain which beverage they would prefer by their side as they read, to make sure that signing pens were available and sobriety was maintained. Although initially Caroline had thought the job would be exotic and exciting, so far it had been largely uneventful, the authors occasionally less than exciting or out-of-sorts from rain, which seemed to show up on event nights as if arranging the chairs in the bookstore was some kind of Pavlovian stimulus for the Pacific Northwest weather. But not much in the way of glamour.

One afternoon, however, a few days after Caroline's coffee date with Marion, the bookstore owner pulled Caroline aside.

"We caught a big one," he said excitedly. "Last minute. He's coming to town to visit friends and he wants a gig so he can write off the trip." He mentioned a name that made Caroline's eyes grow large.

"We'll have to make sure everything is just right," the owner said. "His publicist can't be here, but she said to make sure someone takes him to dinner. And that he eats."

Caroline nodded. The author's preference for liquid meals was material itself for several books.

"You'll take him then?" he asked.

"Me?"

"I can't. My mother-in-law is going to be in town, and I promised I would be home. And we can't get him any other time. But you can do this; it'll be exciting. Just make sure he eats."

Caroline looked nervously across the restaurant table. The Author, as Caroline had come to think of him, was every bit the legend she had imagined from the photos on the back of his numerous books. White hair flew about his head, and he spoke with an erudition that had Caroline mentally counting the clauses in his sentences as if they were mileposts in an effortlessly run marathon.

He had ordered a bottle of red wine before the waitress even handed them their menus, and drained a glass before Caroline could get an hors d'oeuvre, heavy on the protein, to the table. It appeared the only way Caroline could limit his alcohol intake was to drink as much of the bottle as she could. If only it was white wine, Caroline thought, she'd have a better chance. Red wine always made her fuzzy, and she could feel the effects well before the end of her second glass. But the Author seemed happy to carry the conversation; he could talk about anything, it seemed, from inside stories about the vineyard that grew the grapes for the wine they were drinking to the mating habits of dwarf kangaroos.

31

"You know," he commented casually, sitting back and looking at her, a cherry tomato from his salad forgotten on the tines of his upraised fork, "you really are very beautiful."

Caroline registered his words slowly and fought back the immediate urge to correct him, to explain that there were other women, younger women, who were obviously more worthy of the word. Relax, she told herself. The man was old enough to be her father, but it was still a compliment.

"Thank you," she responded, keeping her eyes steadily on her plate. That wasn't so bad, she told herself — embrace the adjective, Caroline. The wine was warm in her chest, the air of the restaurant filled with the heady smells of garlic and butter and oregano. Maybe she *was* beautiful. Take that, Jack.

Plates came and went; at one point Caroline excused herself to use the bathroom and when she returned, the waitress was uncorking a new bottle of wine.

"Oh, we shouldn't," Caroline said to the waitress.

"Too late now," the Author interjected merrily. "Don't worry, little chaperone," he said to Caroline, "I'm a professional."

Caroline quickly checked her watch. An

hour until the book event. She ordered coffee for both of them and cannoli, which she fervently hoped were filled with heavy ricotta. As they were finishing the last bites, she looked about to ask for the check, but their waitress was deeply engrossed talking to another table at the far side of the room.

"So, I was wondering . . ." the Author trailed off. Caroline reluctantly stopped her efforts to attract the waitress and turned her attention to the man across the table from her.

"Perhaps, if you'd be so kind . . ." The Author was motioning to his lap, hidden by the tablecloth.

Years of mothering were hard to overcome. Caroline looked across the table, confused. Had he spilled something? Didn't he have his own napkin?

"Excuse me?" she asked.

"A little stress relief, before the reading?" He smiled at her encouragingly.

"What?"

"Well, I mean, we're getting along so well. I've never had a woman keep up with me on the wine like you have. And the way you lit up when I called you beautiful." Then, more defensively, seeing her expression, "I don't mean right here, of course. Surely you have some atmospheric little alcove back at the store?"

Clarity broke like a plate on the floor. Looking at the Author's confidently expectant expression, Caroline had a sudden memory of Jack confessing about his new girlfriend; the small flicker of pride he couldn't quite hide, the excitement barely simmering under his concern — sincere enough, but honestly a bit late — that he might be hurting her.

She had been so careful to keep things calm, for their son. To be amicable. Accommodating. She had watched her husband walk away from their marriage, taking only what he wanted, leaving behind the rest like a child handing his mother a half-finished ice cream cone on a hot day.

Bastard, she thought suddenly, and felt a pure, bold surge of hatred flash through her body. She looked across the table, straight into the eyes of the Author.

"That's quite an offer," she said, "but I think I've taken care of enough boys in my life."

The reading was over, the Author shoved into his cab. Caroline locked the front door of the store, drove her station wagon around to the back and crammed the trunk full of empty boxes.

When she got home, she hauled the boxes in and stood in the living room, facing the bookshelves. She thought about the day Jack left, the way he packed up his skis and his golf clubs and the nonstick pot he had bought so he could make risotto for her. He had gone out the front door without a glance at the bookshelves. She had followed him to the rental truck parked out front — when did he learn how to rent a truck? she wondered; it had always been she who did things like that — and she asked him if he was coming back for his books.

"My new place is small," he said, with that apologetic shrug of his shoulders she used to find endearing. Then he had gotten in the truck and left.

Now Caroline stood in the living room facing his bookshelf, surrounded by the empty boxes she had brought in from the car. She yanked a four-volume set of Civil War histories from a middle shelf. It left a satisfying hole.

An hour later, Caroline closed the flaps on her fourth box and straightened, feeling the muscles in her lower back and shoulders. It was almost eleven. She walked through the kitchen and out onto the back porch. It was the middle of October, the air chill, its scent a combination of wood smoke and the rain that would come later that night. Caroline shivered slightly and was about to walk back into the warmth of the house, or at least grab the sweater that was hanging over the chair at the kitchen table, when she heard the sound of two low voices in the backyard next door, muffled laughter.

She paused, listening. The neighborhood was close-knit, and there had been a series of break-ins that had everyone watching out for one another even more than usual. She listened, trying to identify the voices, scanning the rhythms of their unintelligible words for patterns she recognized. And then she got it — her teenage neighbor, his girlfriend. Caroline was about to call out so she wouldn't scare them, when she heard the pitch of the laughter change, dropping, low and throaty, adolescent mischief melding into adult need. Voices sliding into languid whispers, becoming urgent, the slow growl of a zipper parting. Caroline leaned against the doorjamb, unable to move.

Her neighbor was a friend, the son only a few years younger than Brad. Caroline had seen the boy come home from the hospital when he was born. She should make a noise and stop the couple, she thought; at the very least, call his mother. And yet she didn't move. Part of her, she understood, didn't want to move, wanted to listen to the seductive rhythm of entreaty and response filtering across the air toward her. She recognized the sounds, missed them in that deep and visceral way that she missed her husband, her life. She heard a soft moan, a quick intake of breath.

Her first night with Jack had been in a hostel in Greece, twenty-five years ago. She hadn't been with anyone before, but she didn't want to tell him, didn't want this glorious boy to turn his gaze to one of the million other girls with backpacks wandering about Europe. She wanted him from the moment she had seen him, a realization as clear and sharp as the intake of her breath when she had gone into the almost hidden anteroom of the church that day and looked up to see the ceiling covered in a mosaic of glittering blues and yellows, a universe made of glass. She had never seen anything like it and it made her stop, awestruck, wishing only that memories were solid objects that you could carry with you. And then there was Jack, entering the door as she exited, all blue eyes and wavy gold hair, and she thought, There you are.

Jack, sneaking into her room in the hostel

after the other girls were asleep, sliding in next to her in the lower bunk, the mattress already warm from waiting, her body and mind utterly awake from willing her roommates to unconsciousness. His fingers running across her in the scratchy twin bed, his touch warm and light, tracing the arc where her forehead met her hair, moving down the length of her arms that she had lazily stretched — was that her? — above her head as he pulled off her shirt, his hands following the curves of her breasts and ribs and waist, sliding over her hip and coming to rest at the final curve of her spine. As her body reached for his she thought, This is why they make ceilings out of colored glass, in tiny rooms that few people will ever enter.

She had seen that expression on his face again a few months ago, when he told her about the new woman, the one he was leaving her for. A longing.

"I love you," he had said. "But Allie — she's still young enough to fall in love. I want to be in love like that."

After that first night in the hostel, Caroline and Jack had traveled together, following each other's whims through the hot streets of Athens, along the beaches of sleepy little fishing villages.

"Come back with me," he had said, as

they lay on the sand one evening, just out of sight of the little cluster of houses that called itself a town. He was about to start a graduate program in economics in Seattle, and Caroline was besotted enough to think of rain as romantic. She didn't want to go home to New England, to her family who would think of her as the girl who had gotten on the plane, a girl she had grown past, like a train overtaking the cars on the highway, heading into mountains and valleys that her family had never seen, wouldn't recognize. Seattle was a rain-washed slate for them to write a life on. And so she went with him.

I grew up with you, Caroline had wanted to tell him, when he said he was leaving her, twenty-five years later. You are a grown-up. But she knew, looking at his face, that it wouldn't make any difference. That it was, perhaps, precisely the point.

Caroline stood on her back porch. The voices near her had hushed, blending in with the movements of the leaves and the quiet caretaking of hands buttoning shirts, adjusting hair.

Caroline leaned against the frame of her back door, waiting for them to leave, touching her cold face with her hands.

■ ■ ■ ■

"I've got a job for you," Caroline told her new trainee at the bookstore the next morning, pointing to the stack of boxes. Caroline's trainee, Annabelle, had the sweet earnestness of a heroine from a Charles Dickens novel; she had not yet learned to take a hard line against textbooks tattooed with yellow and green highlighter marks, or to turn down a sixth copy of *Pride and Prejudice* when three was more than enough. And she was still far more fascinated by the owners than the books in her hands, which was the reason Caroline had been careful to bring in her boxes well before Annabelle's shift started, leaving them in an anonymous stack by the used-book counter.

Annabelle looked at the boxes and her eyes got large, concerned.

"Oh no, did somebody die?"

"Just see what you think they're worth."

"I'm not going to get all these done today," Annabelle said, worried. "The owner asked me to do some inventory work in the new books section."

"That's okay," Caroline said. "They aren't going anywhere." She headed back to the cafe for a cup of coffee.

"I thought you might be working today." Marion walked up to Caroline at the small table in the cafe.

"Come to check up on me?"

"Maybe. I needed a book, too." Marion held up a book; the cover had a photo of a man with an elaborate tattoo running across his shoulder and down his arm. "Research," she said with a smile as she sat down, studying Caroline.

"So how are you doing?" Marion asked her.

"There's a pile of boxes at the used-book desk," Caroline said. "Just don't tell Annabelle they're mine."

"So, progress."

"I suppose. It feels more like carrying out the bodies."

"But you're doing it."

"You know what's going to be hard?" Caroline asked.

"The beach house?"

"Oh, hell," Caroline said, "I haven't even thought of that."

Behind her, Annabelle walked by, a stack of books in her arms.

■ ■ ■ ■

On her way out of the bookstore that afternoon, Caroline saw Annabelle motion to her from the new releases section.

"I got a chance to go through a box or two before I got called over here," Annabelle reported. "There's a *ton* of marketing books. You could sell milk to cows after reading all those."

Caroline nodded and headed out to her car. Jack's marketing books had been a part of her life for so long that she had ceased to register their presence, simply moving them from the couch to the coffee table, from the bed to the nightstand. *How to Sell Everything to Anybody. Eight Great Habits of CEOs.* They all seemed to involve numbers, as if you could simply count yourself to riches, like following sheep to sleep.

Jack hadn't always been like that. When she first met him he had spent hours talking about his studies, fascinated by what he saw as the psychology of humanity playing out in the practicalities of people's lives. His views were wide and expansive, his compassion clear; she had never thought of economics in that way and she found herself thinking that if he could make numbers this exciting, heaven knows what he could do with sex.

Somewhere along the years, things had changed. They both had, she supposed, if she was honest about it. When she had gotten pregnant, Jack started joking that she had become a bird, she was taking the nesting thing so seriously. She turned into the queen of paintbrushes and projects, learning to stencil and buying miniature food grinders so their child could eat only ingredients she had touched herself. She had a stack of cloth diapers ready before the pregnancy was six months along and her fiction reading habits shifted exclusively to books that might have interesting character names she could claim for their child.

She took Jack's jokes with a smile, more than half of it sent, as so many things were those days, inward to the baby inside her. She had even tried to tease Jack in return, commenting on his own new behavior, which was more squirrel-like than avian, as if the world was suddenly filled with impending winter and nuts were few on the ground. But he told her it was important, and so she had dutifully looked over the retirement and college savings plans, the insurance policies for long-term disability. She had listened to his concerns about office politics and his thoughts about how the company could expand and she found herself wondering when the psychology of humanity had turned into a theory of how to get people to buy anything.

It seemed as if these days she was always standing on a stool late at night, Caroline thought as she pulled the last of Jack's books from the top shelf of the bookcase. Caroline heard her cell phone, a rippling of notes she recognized as Kate's ring. But Caroline would have known anyway; no one else would call her this late, not even Brad. Caroline got down from the stool and answered the phone.

Caroline and Kate had met almost twenty years before, a chance encounter at the coffee shop around the corner. Kate had recognized Caroline, who had been trying not to cry while standing in line at the coffee bar near the preschool where the two women had just dropped off their children. Everyone knew Caroline; her son was the howler, the one whose anguished cries at separation spiraled up the staircase of the school building, causing even the nonchalant middle-school students on the second floor to hang their coats a little faster, knock one another on the shoulder before heading into their classrooms. Caroline was the one leaving the preschool classroom with a resolute spine, which folded neatly in half when she reached the front door of the building.

Kate's drop-off at the classroom door was almost embarrassingly brief in comparison, following behind three-year-old Robin, who strode eagerly across the common area, brown paper snack bag held nonchalantly in one tiny hand, eyes aimed forward into the day ahead, into the years when her body would finally grow into the adult she already knew she was. Robin would kiss her mother good-bye and disappear into the glories of a world filled with colored blocks and paints and other children, leaving Kate with hands so empty the only logical solution was a cup of coffee to fill them.

Kate and Caroline had started meeting at the coffee shop regularly on Mondays after drop-off. Mondays were the most likely to fall victim to the inevitable post-weekend crises of forgotten snack items, misplaced laundry and oversleeping — but that only made the coffee at the end of it, the friendly eyes of a compatriot, all the more important.

They had stayed friends over the years, even as their children had gone on to different elementary schools. They counted on each other to hold memories and identities, to remember birthdays and Mother's Days when husbands or children might forget, to be the extra backbone when a hard parenting decision had to be made. The wife's wife, they called each other jokingly, the third support in the three-legged stool that is the unseen structure of many marriages. When Kate and her husband had divorced back when Robin was starting middle school, the bond between the two women had only gotten stronger. So when Kate had called Caroline eighteen months ago after a routine doctor appointment, it had taken Caroline precisely three seconds to know that something was wrong.

In the thousands of calls that had happened since then, Caroline and Kate had worked out a kind of shorthand. Early on, Kate had remarked that even more tiring than chemo were the phone calls with distant friends and relatives, the endless conversations about options and treatments. So Caroline and Kate devised a system; Caroline would call and simply say, "One to ten," and Kate would name a number. "One" would mean Caroline was in the car and headed to Kate's house. "Five" usually meant diversion was on the menu that night

— a story about Caroline's newest book find or a discussion of Robin or Brad's most recent love interest. "Nine" and they were off the phone in two minutes, Kate eager to enjoy the health that was surging, no matter how momentarily, through her body.

It was ironic, Caroline thought; even now with Kate fully in remission, her hair growing longer, thick and radiant, the calls were still one to ten, only now it was Kate calling Caroline, post-Jack.

"One to ten," came Kate's voice over the phone.

"Four and a half," replied Caroline.

"Still angry about your book challenge?"

Caroline laughed. "My house has turned into Box City. What do you think?"

Kate let the phone call unwind into the silence.

"No," Caroline said after a moment. "It was a good idea."

"Okay," said Kate. "You don't have to do this by yourself, you know."

"I know."

When Caroline hung up the phone, she went back into the living room and stood looking at the whiteness of the empty bookcase rising up to the left of the fireplace. Caroline went to her purse and took out the smooth black rock Kate had given her the night of the victory party. Then she walked over to the bookshelf and put the rock on the middle shelf, where it lay small and dark and quiet in the midst of what wasn't there.

Caroline went to the pool the next day, wanting to swim before work, needing to be somewhere simple, clean and blue. She craved the shift that happened when she moved from the loud and echoing world to one of muffled, round quiet, the energy pulsing down her legs as she pushed off the wall, propelling herself forward through the caress of the water until she finally remembered she needed to breathe, and forced herself to surface.

The pool had been Caroline's solace after the chaos and smells of the hospital when Kate was sick. No need to think, just water then air, a quick breath before her face and mind descended gratefully back into the quiet below her. She had started swimming farther and longer, delaying the moment when she would have to leave and return to the world. Occasionally she had missed dinner at home and she was surprised that she cared less than she thought she would. She had declared herself proud when she found that Brad and Jack had figured out a quick meal for themselves, applauding their self-sufficiency when in fact her primary emotion was relief.

After Kate's diagnosis, things had changed between Caroline and Jack. It was as if for Jack bodies had suddenly turned into minefields — liver, lungs, heart, breasts, ovaries, brain — all quietly waiting under the surface to be triggered, blown up. He had started reporting to Caroline with a grim satisfaction about people they knew, even marginally — the neighbor who had collapsed while playing soccer, a coworker's father who had been diagnosed with Alzheimer's. He read articles in the paper about environmental causes for immune diseases, began training for a marathon, brought home giant plastic bottles of supplements with multisyllabic names and insisted she and Brad take them as well.

Caroline had had difficulty being patient — it was she, after all, who sat in the hospital, who held Kate as she retched into the toilet, watched death tease and poke at her friend like some schoolyard bully. And suddenly she had been frustrated, angered even, by her husband's seeming inability to take care of himself. The things she used to do for him and take such pleasure in now were all signs of his own inadequacy. Make your own damn coffee, she wanted to say, and she had been shocked at the sound of the voice in her head, its sharp, mean edge.

Now, as Caroline swam through the water of the pool, from the back of her mind came something Jack had said during their one truly horrible fight. Kate had had a bad reaction to chemo that day, and after Caroline left the hospital she went to the pool. She came home late, without calling. Jack had met her at the door and informed her, his voice tight, that she'd missed dinner. She yelled, told him he was selfish; she was on the front line, she said, not him.

Jack had looked at her, the anger in his eyes turning into sadness. It's only called a front line, he said, if there's another one behind it.

When Caroline arrived at the bookstore that afternoon, her hair still damp from the pool, she could feel the change in the air. An author event was scheduled for that evening, another big name, and the bookstore was already seeing an increased traffic flow as word got around. Anticipatory cache, Caroline called it.

As the time approached, Caroline stood at the front door, welcoming customers and directing them back to the cafe area where the tables and chairs had been rearranged to accommodate a large crowd. The author wasn't there yet, but Caroline had gotten used to late entrances during her stint as coordinator, had even gotten to the point where she smiled a bit to herself at the newly minted authors who showed up the requested fifteen minutes early.

Her cell phone rang and Caroline looked down, seeing a number she didn't recognize. She opened her phone.

"This is Mary." The publicist — not a good sign. "I just got a call. She's not coming. One of her characters died unexpectedly today. She says she's in mourning and can't see anyone."

"I have a roomful of people here."

"And I wish I had an author for you." The publicist's own exasperation simmered beneath their mutual knowledge of the author's sales record.

"What am I supposed to do?"

"Can you tap-dance? Seriously — I'm sorry; I owe you one." And the phone call ended with a click.

The glamour might not yet be apparent in her job, Caroline thought. But drama, there was plenty. She headed back to the cafe.

■ ■ ■ ■

"I'm sorry," Caroline announced to the assembled crowd. "It appears our author will not be able to make it tonight."

There was a shifting in seats, a disgruntled murmuring.

"I want to thank you all for coming, anyway," Caroline finished lamely.

"Wait, that's it?" Annabelle, Caroline's trainee, stood in the back of the room, a portrait of dismayed innocence.

"Well. . . ." Surely they wouldn't want her to tap-dance.

"We can do better than that," Annabelle said.

Caroline raised a questioning eyebrow; the crowd turned to Annabelle.

"What if . . ." Annabelle cast about for ideas, and then proceeded with excitement. "What if we don't need an author for a reading? What if *we* read? I mean, maybe not *her* book, that might be a little strange, but we could read other ones, right?"

The crowd shifted, some of the customers gathering their things and leaving, but others leaning forward in their chairs, interested, listening. Annabelle looked to Caroline for reassurance; Caroline shrugged and smiled.

"Okay," Annabelle said determinedly. She pointed to Caroline and two regular customers from the crowd. "We four will each go find our favorite passage from a favorite book. Everybody else can buy coffee or cookies or something and we'll reconvene in a few minutes."

The espresso machine steamed into action; the cash register opened with a satisfying pop of commerce. Caroline headed into the aisles, searching for her selection. A favorite book. A favorite passage. She passed the coming-of-age novel that had spoken to her as a college student, a memoir that had been given to her when she was a young mother, the one that told her she was not alone. Books that had arrived in her life over the years like playmates, or a loving grandmother, a slightly wicked boyfriend. More family than family, some of them.

She thought of the people waiting to hear her selection. She felt a responsibility; she was in charge of the event, after all. What would they think of her choice? What would make them happy? Her hand pulled back from the Elizabeth Gaskell novel she had been about to take from the shelf, reached instead for the recent release she knew was a favorite among the bookstore's clientele. They had hand-sold hundreds of copies over the past year. The critics loved it; the narrator was opinionated, the language quick and bright.

She walked back to the microphone, where the other three readers were waiting. The crowd reassembled in their chairs, laughing as they tried to balance coffee cups and plates with cookies.

"Now," announced Annabelle, "we're going to try something we do in my family when we are playing poker. We call it 'pass the trash,' but I think we'll probably have to give it a new name here."

"What?" said the man standing next to her.

"We are each going to pass our selection to the person to our right. That way we'll read through someone else's eyes. It'll be more fun."

Annabelle turned to Caroline and pushed a book, its pages opened, into her hands.

"Here," Annabelle said, pointing to a passage. Caroline's eyes instinctively took in the words.

. . . And then, some morning in the second week, the mind wakes, comes to life again. Not in a city sense — no — but beach-wise. It begins to drift, to play, to turn over in gentle careless rolls like those lazy waves on the beach. One never knows what chance treasures these easy unconscious rollers may toss up, on the smooth white sand of the conscious mind; what perfectly rounded stone, what rare shell from the ocean floor . . .

Caroline looked up and saw Annabelle watching her, a smile on her face.

The crowd was gone, their excited voices disappearing into the night. The evening had been a great success; after the four read their selections the event devolved into a kind of friendly free-for-all, customers hopping out of their chairs and picking books, passing them on to strangers and friends, reading aloud into the microphone. More events were planned for the future.

Caroline was rearranging the chairs; Annabelle had found the broom and followed behind her, chasing crumbs. She was humming under her breath, a contented, happy song.

"So, did you know . . . ?" Caroline asked. Annabelle looked up, her eyes clear and innocent.

"That those are your husband's books I've

55

been going through all week? Yes."

"How?"

"Caroline." Annabelle sounded older suddenly, amused. "It's a bookstore. We specialize in stories."

When Caroline got home, she picked up the phone and called Marion.

"I'm going to the beach house," she said. "Will you come with me?"

Caroline and Jack had found the beach house more than twenty years before, on a camping trip they took to celebrate Jack's completion of graduate school. Money had been tight — Jack about to start his first real job, student loans still competing with grocery money. But there *was* a job, an offer so grown-up and full of possibility that it felt as if the door to adulthood had opened to reveal a candy store; and as they drove along the coast that day, looking for the campground, Jack was planning the big house they would have someday, the safe and clean neighborhood they would live in.

It was Caroline who spotted the collection of wind-battered cottages clustered along the beach like abandoned oyster shells. They reminded her of the philosophical and religious retreats she had seen on the East

Coast when she was growing up, each little house an almost-twin of the next, the very smallness of their size quieting physical movement, inviting contemplation.

As their car passed the first of the houses, Caroline had seen a sign and begged Jack to stop. And while he had been worried about reaching the campground in time to claim a good site, he smiled at the excitement in her voice and pulled over.

Caroline looked more closely at the sign when she got out of the car.

"Jack," she said. "They're for sale — all of them!"

They had strolled along the row of abandoned cottages like Goldilocks choosing a bed, pretending they had all the money in the world and possession was merely a matter of preference. The first cottage was too close to the road; the next was not quite angled correctly to take full advantage of the view, they had agreed, delighting in the maturity of their insights. They walked, holding hands, until they reached the end of the row where they saw a cottage set a bit farther apart, looking across a dune to the water.

"That's the one," Caroline said, pointing, and Jack laughed.

When they walked around the back, they

had found an unlocked window, and after a moment's hesitation they pushed it open, the wood of the window squealing against the frame. Jack boosted Caroline and she scrambled through, feeling like a nine-year-old. As she walked through the house to the front door to let Jack in, she breathed in, expecting dust and mold, but was greeted instead by the smell of fresh sheets and sunshine that seemed to come from the walls themselves.

She had gazed around her at the tiny rooms, at the windows that would open, she knew, to sand and water and sky. The light shimmered through the tattered lace of the curtains, played along the ridges of the faded white ship-lath walls.

"I'll take care of you," she said aloud.

She had opened the front door, her face radiant, and pulled Jack inside. They made love on the rag rug that had been left on the living room floor. Six months later, on Caroline's birthday, she opened an envelope to find the deed to the cottage inside.

They had cleaned and painted, replaced the cracked window in the bedroom, scavenged furniture from garage sales. Over time, people had bought the other cottages and a community of sorts had developed, neighbors you could ask for sugar or lighter fluid when the only store, some five miles away, just felt too far. Their son had grown up spending stormy winter weekends at the cottage and as much of the summers as Jack's schedule could accommodate. By the age of five Brad could imitate a seagull with stunning accuracy; by ten he could catch any Frisbee thrown the length of the beach. They had celebrated birthdays and anniversaries here, hosted an annual summer party where friends from the city pitched tents on the beach and gathered around a fire pit on late August evenings when the light stayed in the sky until ten at night and the stories went on longer than any child was supposed to be awake.

As important as the cottage had been to them when Brad was young, the frequency of their visits had stalled out almost completely when he went to high school. He had things to do, Brad told them, and Jack had said they should encourage his independence. Caroline didn't fight it; she was busy taking care of Kate and working. Then came the time last November, when Caroline had come to the cottage for a weekend with Kate and found a book she didn't recognize on her bed stand, and she finally realized whose independence Jack had been wanting to encourage.

■ ■ ■ ■

The row of cottages was uninhabited when Caroline and Marion turned off the main road. Although it was the end of October, Caroline had arranged her work schedule so they could come mid-week when encounters with the neighbors would be less likely. Even more so than their neighborhood in Seattle, the beach community was close-knit, partly by necessity but also because their bonds had been made when they were their most relaxed — what they thought of as their best — selves. As much as the sight of the ocean and sand meant vacation, so, too, did the vision that they saw of themselves in their neighbors' eyes. I am that person, they would think, and shoulders would loosen, shoes would slide off feet.

Caroline had chosen their cottage for its relative privacy, but over the years, as the other cottages had been bought and filled with people and furniture and laughter, that first trip down the pathway from the car to their cottage, arms filled with suitcases and grocery bags, had become like walking a long welcome line, neighbors calling out invitations to dinner, children clamoring for

Brad to dump his stuff, now, and come and play.

There had been other divorces, cottages divided into his and her weekends, or sold immediately. They had all sold eventually, family traditions unraveling until there seemed little point in keeping the walls that had held them. When Jack had told her he was leaving, he said the cottage was hers — and while she tried to see that as a generous act, she couldn't rid herself of the vision of Brad's older cousin who had always made a grand gesture of giving Brad a favorite toy when the wheel was already broken.

It's not the cottage I want, she had almost said, but stopped herself because there was a chance Jack might take her literally.

It was a strange thing about the cottage, Caroline had remarked once. They could paint walls or cook crabs, have a fire in the fireplace or burn a batch of cookies while distracted by a sunset. Still, every time she returned, she was greeted by the same smell of fresh sheets and sunshine that had been there the first time, as if the house itself had a natural scent that it rediscovered each time they were gone.

"I love this place," Marion said as she dropped her suitcase by the front door and carried a bag of groceries to the kitchen.

It was the first time Caroline had been back since the book by her bed told her what Jack hadn't. She hadn't stayed that time, couldn't sleep in the bed; she and Kate had checked into a hotel fifteen miles down the road and spent the weekend not thinking about how their lives had turned out differently than they expected.

"Wine?" called Marion from the kitchen.

Marion had insisted upon candles with dinner, the light flickering off the glass of the windows.

"Somebody told me once about burning sage to chase out the old spirits," she said, "but I like the idea of candles better. They go so much better with dinner."

They had cooked together in the small kitchen, moving around each other with the grace of long friendship, Caroline picking up and cutting the carrot that Marion had just peeled, Marion stirring the chicken in the sauté pan while Caroline added the onions, followed by tomatoes. Marion had brought the last of the oregano from her garden and the dusty-sweet smell filled the house when it touched the warmed oil. Caroline cut thick slices of bread, bought from the bakery near her house, and scattered the carrots across the top of the salad. Marion pulled the bottles of olive oil and vinegar from the cupboard, drizzling dressing across the lettuce, finishing with a few firm pulls from the salt grinder. As Caroline put the plates on the table, she realized it had been a long time since she had cooked anything. For months now, the only food she had been able to get her hands to take off the grocery store shelves had been rice pudding and canned chicken spread, the reasons for her choices as baffling as pregnancy cravings.

But when the first bite met her mouth, it was as if her body suddenly remembered food, and she found herself taking a second helping, another slice of bread, a third glass of wine. They ate, their conversation weaving back and forth across the table, filling the house with fresh news, old stories. Finally, the food was gone, the last of the wine poured into glasses, only the dishes left.

Caroline took a long, slow swallow, looking toward the darkened window.

"So, why do you think people do it?" she asked. "Leave each other?"

"I don't know," Marion answered.

"But you've written articles about it."

"That doesn't mean I know anything."

Marion's tone was light. Caroline looked over at her, waiting. After a while, Marion gestured out toward the ocean beyond the windows.

"I think love is kind of like those waves out there," she said. "You ride one in to the beach, and it's the most amazing thing you've ever felt. But at some point the water goes back out; it has to. And maybe you're lucky — maybe you're both too busy to do anything drastic. Maybe you're good as friends, so you stay. And then something happens — maybe it's something as big as a baby, or as small as him unloading the dishwasher — and the wave comes back in again. And it does that, over and over. I just think sometimes people forget to wait."

The next morning came gray and cool. Caroline woke up on the couch, her back stiff, and walked into the kitchen where Marion was making coffee.

"You're a little twitchy this morning," Marion remarked as she took a coffee mug out of the cupboard. "Want some?"

"Thanks," Caroline answered, adding, "It was easier back at the house."

"Sure." Marion poured out two cups, put sugar in hers, and then drank deeply and with great satisfaction.

"Okay," she said when she had finished. "Where's the book?"

"What do you mean?"

"*Her* book," Marion repeated, looking at her sideways. "I know you. It's here somewhere; you haven't gotten rid of it, have you?"

Caroline went into the bedroom and pulled a paperback off the shelf in the closet. The cover had a title draped across a gauzy photograph of red, high-heeled shoes.

"Original," murmured Marion, one eyebrow raised. "Okay, come with me."

Marion walked out the front door and down the pathway, past the closed window blinds and doors of the neighboring cottages, to the parking area. She lifted the lid of the large blue dumpster.

"Pitch it," she said.

"But . . ."

"I know; it's a book. Pitch it."

Caroline hesitated, and then with an instinctive motion up and over, her arm pulled back and launched the book into the air. It landed with a satisfying thump at the bottom of the empty dumpster.

"Good girl," said Marion. "Now, I'm going to take a walk. You can box up the rest."

There were not as many books here as in

the city, Caroline thought as she ran her eyes around the living room of the cottage, but the arrangement was more casual, Jack's and Brad's books intermixed with hers on the shelves, tossed on coffee tables, hidden in the couch cushions. She couldn't even tell for sure whose was whose sometimes. The cottage was where Jack had brought his favorite childhood books — *Harold and the Purple Crayon, Robinson Crusoe, Huckleberry Finn.* Caroline remembered winter evenings cooking dinner in the kitchen, hearing the sound of Jack's voice reading aloud, or later, Brad's voice reading to his father.

What should she do with the children's books? They were Brad's as much as his father's — and the thought that Jack might want them for future children made Caroline want to start a fire in the woodstove and feed it with words. But should she save them for Brad? And what would those books mean to him now? Brad's response to his father's leaving had been abrupt and angry, his attitude toward his mother protective. Caroline still got her son's cell phone bill; there were no records of calls to his father.

But Brad and his father had been close before, especially at the cottage. They had all been different here, she thought as she looked around the room, their roles softened, melded, the need for efficiency falling away with every mile they traveled from the city. During those times, Brad didn't belong to her, Jack didn't belong to work; they all had simply belonged to each other.

She understood what Marion had been talking about the night before, about marriage; it made more sense here in this place than anywhere. Over the years of her marriage, she had experienced that ebb and swell of feeling many times. The dry days, when life with Jack was one more item on her to-do list, followed by the return of something so familiar, the gratitude she had always experienced along with a start of recognition — oh yes, *that* was what it felt like; how could she have forgotten? So often, she had felt her love for her husband return here at the cottage, in a moment when she would see Jack look up from a puzzle, or come in to help her put sheets on their bed.

Yet somewhere along the line, she had always forgotten again. And over the years she had forgotten it more quickly, easily, until even the loveliest gestures, the ones that might have brought the emotion flowing in to shore — the way Jack washed her car every Sunday so she could start the week fresh, the way she always brought him coffee while he took a shower — merged with all the other ones — his steadfast ability to sleep through the sound of a crying baby, her inability to leave on a trip without turning back twice to check for stove burners left on — all those tics and traits stored in the house that was their marriage, overrunning the space, piling up against the door like solicitations until, yes, the desire simply to walk away and leave them behind was almost overwhelming. Almost. Because the one thing she could never forgive Jack for was the way he had blown open the door of their marriage first and left. Jack-in-the-box, turning his own handle, springing up and out, hands free.

Caroline worked steadily, sorting through belongings, filling boxes. By the time she was finished, it was late afternoon; Marion had come back from her walk long before and had gone out for groceries. Caroline grabbed one last paperback, left on top of the refrigerator — a thriller, the kind Jack had been reading the past few years. A piece of paper fell out from between the pages. She picked it up and looked at it, and again more closely. A biopsy report. Type: Prostate. Results: Negative.

Caroline scanned the paper for the date and found it at the top of the page. September, a little over a year ago. Kate had been five months into her chemotherapy.

Caroline stared at the date. She hadn't known. That simple fact could mean so many different things about her husband, their relationship, and she realized as she stood in the kitchen of their cottage that it had been years since she could have said with any certainty which one was true. Gently, she put the paper into the front of the book and laid it back on top of the refrigerator. Then she took the last of the boxes out to the car.

Marion and Caroline sat in the front porch chairs watching the light disappear from the sky, blankets around their shoulders, the air chill on their faces. Marion looked over at Caroline.

"You've done good work," Marion said. "Come sit in front of me and I'll work on your shoulders."

Caroline gratefully moved over in front of Marion's chair. Marion had taken classes when she was writing an article about the various massage schools in town and it turned out she had a real gift, but she had simply laughed at the idea of trading journalism for massage.

"I'll just give to my friends," she had said, and she had been good as her word. Kate had said the one upside of chemotherapy was Marion afterward.

Marion placed her hands on Caroline's shoulders and held them there, pushing down gently, firmly. Caroline's shoulders relaxed, her chin lifted.

"You had a big day. You doing okay?" Marion asked.

Caroline nodded. She sat, eyes closed, feeling Marion's hands find their way into muscles, her fingers moving gently, searching as if they could hear something ears could not.

When was the last time, Caroline wondered, that Jack had touched her, she had touched him, like this — a natural overflow of affection, as simple and essential as water? It had been like this early on, Jack's fingers resting for a moment on her lower back, her cheek, as he passed by.

When their son was born, so early, the doctor had said that massage was important; it would help him grow, be able to go home sooner. Caroline had sat by Brad's bassinet in the hospital, her fingers moving in small circles over his chest, in soft, long sweeps down his bird-bone legs and arms, love

70

flowing through her fingers into his body. Stay with me, stay with me, stay with me. Her life reduced to one child, two hands, hers.

It had been three weeks before they could bring Brad home, to a house that Jack left every morning, his parental leave long since used up, leaving Caroline in a cashmere world of skin. She would watch Jack get dressed, buttoning, zipping, buckling, while she lay cocooned in bed with the baby. What could touch you in a land of metal elevators and wooden desks, when all that was uncovered were hands, a face? She, who spent her days in bare feet and a bathrobe, living skin to skin with another human being, could not imagine at the time. Did not even think about it, her own world so full that any human being besides her baby was at best an appendage in her life.

But now, she wondered. How cold it must have been in all those clothes.

When was the last time she and Jack had really touched each other? Maybe that's what Jack had meant when he talked about wanting to be in love — not just hands on skin, but that feeling of being seen, understood. Maybe it had just become too hard, with all those lawns to mow and grocery lists, all the accumulated roles of their lives between them.

But sitting there on the porch, Caroline realized with a sense of small quiet surprise that the roles in her well-stocked bookshelf of life were leaving, had left, one by one as they had come. Kate was healthy again. Brad still called home for his mother-fixes, as he called them, but he was no longer the reason for Caroline's life. Cooking and cleaning were simpler now, fertility, or not, no longer an issue. She knew how she liked to dress, didn't spend a lot of time worrying or shopping. And now she was no longer a wife — all the caretaking slipping away, leaving her weightless, open.

There was an almost literary irony, she thought now, in how Jack had gone rampaging through his life this year, cleaning the shelves in one sweep, when the reality was they were already emptying, quietly and efficiently, on their own. Searching for a clean slate, he had chosen a woman at the beginning of her adult life, who would want to fill shelves again with children and diaper bags and strollers, more baggage than you could ever carry on. He had jumped out of the cycle only to go back to the beginning, filling his hands again.

Marion's thumb moved to the inside of Caroline's left shoulder blade, following the line of the bone, reaching in to the muscles below.

"Too much?" Marion asked.

"No," Caroline answered. Behind her the last rays of the sun reached into the living room, lighting the walls blue and gold.

DARIA

One time, almost two years ago, Daria's older sister Marion had given her a gallon-sized Ziploc bag filled with off-white goo. The over-Xeroxed instructions called it "Amish Friendship Bread." It was so easy, the instructions declared — mush the bag, mush the bag, mush the bag. Add some water and flour and sugar. Mush again. Make more starter, give new bags of goo to three of your friends, and bake your bread. Stunningly simple. You can do it, Marion had said supportively; you might have fun.

It was a chain letter camouflaged as food, Daria could see that. It even came with a peppy little note like all the chain letters in junior high: "Pass this on to three friends. If you do, your dearest wish will come true. If you don't, you will fall to earth in a plane crash/suffer a heart attack/lose the love of your life." Those letters were always threats dressed in smiles, the epistolary equivalent of a head cheerleader. Daria hated them, deeply and viscerally — their cheerful theft of your time, their assumption that you had three friends.

Daria had taken the goo-bag home, held between two fingers like a wet diaper, and pitched it onto the kitchen counter. In the morning she noticed that bubbles had surreptitiously formed in the bag during the night, lightening the humorless quality of the starter. Bubbles. All on their own, without her help. She mushed the bag, feeling the goo beneath the plastic give under her fingers, a bit like clay, but smoother, looser. The next morning the same, and the next, opening the seal and letting out the air each time, then closing the bag, gently and firmly, like a mother tucking a reluctant child into bed. Maybe there wasn't so much to that baking thing after all.

On the fourth morning she walked into the kitchen, flicked on the switch for the coffeepot and looked over at her burbling little friend. The edgy, fecund smell of yeast tickled the air, mingling with the earthy aroma of the percolating coffee. She reached over and gave the bag a squeeze, an affectionate foreshadowing of mushing to come, at which point the seal, not entirely secured from the previous release of air, popped open and goo vomited across the counter, trickling over the edge, oozing into a partially opened drawer and dropping onto the floor in round, soft splats.

Shit, thought Daria. She scraped the goo back into the bag, wondering what fermentation aids were lingering on the average kitchen counter, and stored the whole mess on top of the refrigerator. It sat there throughout the day, morose, guilt-inducing, occasionally emitting a small, pathetic bubble to call her attention to its fate. She'd had boyfriends who were subtler. She was about to go on a trip, anyway, a weekend with a man she barely knew, the excitement of the date enough without adding the guilt bread. Maybe she could let the stuff die now. It couldn't possibly live through such a traumatic experience.

What was the point, anyway? She wasn't Amish. She liked cars and bread from the store, and the way a zipper could slide open down your back in the right man's hands. She wasn't her mother, the bread-making queen. Her dishes didn't match, because she made them herself — not that her mother ever seemed that impressed with Daria's pottery. Why did you have to prove you could bake bread when you made the plates you served it on?

But the next day, when the starter still miraculously burbled, she had relented and the plastic bag accompanied her on the weekend getaway, sitting in the backseat of the man's car between their overnight bags like a small nervous child with a gastrointestinal disorder, surrounded by paper towels in case of eruption.

"Really?" the man she barely knew had asked.

"You said you liked me for my unpredictability," she answered.

"Really?" he repeated.

The guilt-goo survived longer than the relationship, arriving home with Daria on Sunday evening. The car had been cold on the drive back but the starter seemed to be doing a better job of coping with the weekend than she was, even though once she read the directions she realized she was supposed to have made bread from it the day before. The stuff was impressive, Daria had to admit as she held the bag in her hands.

Sitting on her kitchen table was her grandmother's bowl, creamy white inside, crimson on the exterior. Daria remembered the first time she had seen the bowl at her grandmother's house when she was a child, how the sun coming in the back kitchen window lit up the deep red of the glaze and nestled in the ridges running up the sides, how she had gotten her hand lightly slapped for trying to sneak batter, when all she had done was reach out to feel the smooth surface, the edge of a ridge pressed against her finger. When her grandmother had died a few years earlier, Daria refused all objects from her house, claiming she didn't have space in her tiny apartment, anyway. But as she had passed through her grandmother's house while the other relatives were still talking in the backyard, she saw the bowl on the kitchen counter and took it.

Guilt bread made in a stolen bowl, Daria thought wryly. She divided the starter into four parts and poured one portion into the bowl.

The goo looked a bit gray, and Daria had already put in baking soda before she realized it should have been powder, but she put the whole thing in a loaf pan and dumped some cinnamon across the top and stuck it in the oven — from which it emerged forty minutes later, fragrant, lovely and forgiving.

So why did she have to do it all again now? Daria thought, mulling over Kate's challenge. Hadn't she already proved herself? She'd even taken Kate half the loaf of the

Amish guilt bread — on a plate she had made herself, red for healing power.

Sometimes, Daria thought, that group of women was more trouble than it was worth. She'd only said yes to the do-one-thing-that-scares-you pact because she thought she would get something exciting like bungee jumping or sex on a houseboat. She should have known better. Kate hated boats. "Learn how to make bread" — that was classic Kate.

Standing in her pottery studio, Daria ripped open the plastic on a package of clay and got ready to prep it.

Daria always told people that unpredictability was her birthright, earned by her unanticipated conception on the night of her sister Marion's sixteenth birthday party. Daria had often wondered what could have prompted her mother into such a display of sexual recklessness, as it was obvious to Daria early on that love or the desire to look down into the clear gaze of a baby's eyes had had nothing to do with it. Maybe it had been all those lanky teenage bodies, sending their hormones ricocheting about the house. Despite all evidence to the contrary, Daria liked the idea that there might at least have been something passionate in her creation.

Not that she was ever likely to ask her mother.

Daria often referred to her mother as the patron saint of perpetual disappointment. Daria envisioned her, arms outspread, welcoming the hordes of the ticked off, the judgmental, the depressed, into her all-encompassing embrace, where she would teach them essential life skills such as how to take the silver lining out of clouds, or conjure flaws out of thin air. Daria had overheard her mother telling friends how the labor with her second daughter was like birthing a cactus — the implication clear to Daria that things had not changed in the intervening years.

Daria took a sharp wire with a wooden handle on each end and sliced through the cool, hard block of clay in front of her. She picked up a chunk, testing its weight in her hands, feeling its moist surface clinging to her skin. Then she cupped her hands around it and shoved down, hard, onto the board with the heel of her hand, her thumbs. She pulled the red-brown mass off the board with the ends of her fingers, pivoting it toward her, pushing again with all her strength, feeling the energy move from her shoulders through her elbows, down her

80

forearms to the clay. Push, flip, push, flip, pressing out the air that would cause a pot to explode in the kiln.

It was Marion whom Daria remembered when she thought of her childhood. Marion, already owning the sensual, sand-dune lines of breasts and hips and thighs by the time Daria was born, taking Daria out into the world with a grown-up assurance that was both a relief and entirely frustrating to Daria. When she was young, Daria always thought that the glasses Marion wore were special, allowing her to read the road signs in life that were incomprehensible to Daria — the line forming between their mother's eyes, a smile from an aunt or uncle that might or might not be friendly, the inflection in a shopkeeper's voice.

It was Marion who had told Daria the story of the chocolate cake Marion made herself for her sixteenth birthday party, a tower of three dirt-dark layers and luxurious brown frosting. A taste of that cake had magical effects, Marion had told Daria, as wonderful as the bite of Snow White's apple had been disastrous. In Marion's tale, Daria's conception became art, created by a kind of glorious, dark chocolate fate.

But when Daria was five, Marion left the

Midwest and moved to Seattle, taking her stories and her special glasses with her, and Daria gave up trying to read the road signs of life. It seemed much simpler to become something for the world to navigate around, rather than the reverse.

It wasn't difficult. Daria already attracted attention with her tumbleweed hair and desire to play in the mud, her preemptive strikes on the playground, her unusual eating habits, which changed and developed over the years. There was the time when she was six and decided to eat only one color per week, following the order of the rainbow (yellow by far the easiest, particularly if you were allowed to include tan). Twelve was the year of vegetarianism; fifteen, the stage when her body started following the curves of her older sister, a time of green protein shakes and strenuous gustatory self-denial.

What was considered odd in elementary and junior high school became an asset on the dating circuit later in life. Men always loved the hummingbirds, weightless and colorful, so quick you could never catch them even if you wanted to. And her affinity for mud had turned into a profession in clay.

Daria had first encountered clay the summer she turned ten, when her mother signed her up for arts and crafts camp. The fact that Daria's mother — who was eternally and vocally annoyed at Daria's love of playing in mud — was willing to spend good money when it was called clay was highly amusing to Daria, who wisely said nothing and even expressed a few carefully timed expressions of reluctance to make sure her mother didn't change her mind.

But the moment Daria touched clay, her hands instinctively wrapped around the ball the teacher had given her. It was like mud you could control, flexible, warmed by your hands, made slick with water. She spent the first day rhythmically flattening her ball into a circle, then rolling it up into the roundest shape she could create, feeling the silkiness of its surface against the skin of her palms, the calming weight in her hands. She listened barely, dreamily, to the teacher explain the origin of clay, imagining the particles letting go of the big rocks and rolling downstream, flattening, smoothing out, blending with others. She wondered where her clay had wandered from, which river it had floated down, what made it stop and settle. The teacher was calling clay common, but Daria knew better. Every particle in her hands came from somewhere, traveled to somewhere else. There was nothing common about that; it didn't matter that they were cast off in the first place.

Even now, every time Daria soaked the hard scraps from previous projects and watched them turn back into wet clay, she marveled at how infinitely forgiving her medium was. Up until the time it was placed in the kiln, any pot could be sent back to its beginning, any mark could be undone, the final piece holding all its iterations within itself while displaying only the final one.

As Daria cut and wedged her last chunk of clay for the day, she heard her cell phone ring. Rinsing and wiping her hands, she reached over and opened the phone, seeing Sara's number on the screen. Daria and Sara had met a few years earlier, when Sara's twins were only a few weeks old. Marion had organized a baby-holding circle, to give Sara a chance to use one of her arms for something other than cradling a baby, Marion had said. Daria was not a big fan of babies — in her experience, they tended to crawl on the floor and eat clay — but Marion had insisted Daria join the group, saying they needed five people, one for each day of the week when Sara's husband was at work. And even though Daria and Sara were completely different — Sara quintessentially domestic, tied to her three children and her house and her husband — Daria couldn't help liking her. There was just something so genuinely friendly about Sara, and her children's Halloween costumes were something you didn't want to miss. Daria always thought Sara would make a wonderful artist, if she'd just stop making peanut butter sandwiches.

"Daria?" Sara's voice on the phone sounded more excited than Daria had heard it in a long time. "I have someone here you have to meet. Can you come for dinner tonight?"

Sara's kitchen was a chicken farm of chaos, the twins, Max and Hillary, sitting in booster seats at the kitchen table, board books and grapes and crackers spread about them, seven-year-old Tyler's soccer shoes dripping mud in the center of the floor. Sara negotiated the obstacles unconsciously, her eyes on the children, the ingredients for the meal she was preparing. Daria stood at the kitchen island, tearing lettuce leaves for a salad.

"So, who is it I'm supposed to meet?" Daria asked. Sara pulled a cooking tray of chicken strips out of the microwave and arranged them on plates. The twins whooped in anticipation.

"You remember me talking about my brother, Henry?" Sara's voice was lit with happiness. "He's been traveling for years, but he's in town now for a while."

Daria had heard about the elusive Henry, Sara's twin brother, the one who left home with a backpack after college and returned only sporadically for a dose of family before heading out to a new country whose language he didn't speak, a culture whose food he'd never tried. Last Daria had heard, Henry was in Peru, but you never knew. Postcards sometimes took months to arrive, and Henry was not a big believer in email. His last stint had been long enough that he had yet to meet Sara's own twins.

"What does he think of the rug rats?" Daria motioned toward the twins at the kitchen table.

"They adore him, of course. He let them go through his backpack. There were presents. I'll never be able to keep them out of my luggage now," Sara said. "If I travel," she added ruefully, efficiently knocking the lid of an applesauce jar with the side of a knife and popping the seal. Outside, the sound of steps moved across the gravel path toward the kitchen.

"Okay, darlings," she said, moving aside

the board books. "Time for dinner. Uncle Henry is here with the milk."

Daria looked up as the back door opened. She didn't know why she had expected Henry to look as if he was a boy just out of college; maybe it was all the stories Sara told about when they were younger. But the man in front of her was in his mid-thirties, slim and dark, with a quiet stillness about him that seemed to pool in his eyes. He moved across the kitchen with a grace like his sister's but with none of the tiredness, ruffling Max and Hillary's hair as he passed, and handed Sara the carton of milk. His jeans were old, his T-shirt older.

"Yummmmm . . ." he said, smiling at the twins. "Chicken fingers."

He turned to Daria and held out his hand. "I'm Henry."

"Daria." He smelled like warm wheat fields and wine.

"What can I do to help?" Henry asked, turning to his sister.

"Help Daria finish up that salad, and once Dan is home from work, we'll eat."

Daria moved slightly to make room for Henry at the kitchen island. He slipped into place next to her and picked up the knife, making a series of quick, controlled slices down the length of a carrot. Daria watched it fall open into a row of neat circles.

"Short-order cook?" Daria asked.

"Sometimes. When I need to. Mostly I'm a baker."

"A baker? Really? As in bread?" Daria shot a look across the kitchen to Sara, who grinned and ducked her head.

"Uhm hmm." Henry picked up a radish and a smaller knife. With a few deft strokes he turned it into a rose and handed it to Hillary, causing Max to clamor for his own.

"Troublemaker," Sara commented affectionately. "Daria, why don't you get Henry out of my way and show him your work. Daria makes these incredible pots, Henry; she's getting really well known. I've got one of them on the bookshelf in the family room."

"Not very subtle, is she?" Daria commented as they went into the next room. She pulled the pot off one of the upper shelves, where it had been placed far out of the reach of the children. It rested, barely contained in her palms, its shape a reverse hourglass. Tendrils of green and blue swam on the surface, memories of seaweed and sky.

"It's lovely," Henry said, taking it into his own hands. "It reminds me of an octopus pot, only much smaller."

"Exactly," Daria said, surprised. "How did you know?"

"I remember seeing these long lines of them, pulled up on the beach in Greece."

"He's a real water freak," Sara called from the kitchen. "Ask him where he is living, Daria."

"Where are you living, Henry?" Daria asked dutifully.

"Down in the marina, off Eastlake."

"You live on a houseboat?"

"I'm boat-sitting. A friend of mine is traveling for a year." He laughed at the excitement on her face. "Why? Do you want to see it sometime?"

"Why a baker?" Daria asked. She and Henry were sitting in folding chairs on the deck of the houseboat in their heaviest coats and scarves, watching their breath fan out into the darkness. It was well past midnight; the noises from the other houseboats had quieted, the only lights from the porches, illuminating the small ripples shivering across the lake.

"Why a potter?" he countered.

"I asked you first."

"Well, I like mornings." He laughed at her expression. "Really. It started the first time I was driving across the States. It's so much easier to be on the road before everyone else. And the light, the way the sun comes up across the fields in the Midwest and just defines every cornstalk; it's really beautiful."

Daria nodded. It was one of the few things she missed about where she had grown up.

"Anyway, I ran out of money in this little seaport in Massachusetts. I didn't have any baking experience, but I was willing to get up early and they needed a dough mixer. And I liked it. There's something about getting up at four in the morning that's different than staying up all night. I liked walking down the middle of a road if I wanted, looking up at the moon. And I liked being the first person in the bakery, turning on the ovens, measuring out the flour and the water, smelling the yeast. I liked the idea that I was making a day out of such simple ingredients."

He looked out over the water. Daria hugged her knees against the cooling air.

"Why a potter?" he asked after a while. "Your turn."

Daria's answer was quick, practiced. "I like to play with mud." She laughed, the sound bouncing off the surface of the lake.

Henry stayed quiet for a while. "You know," he said musingly after a few moments, "I never met anyone who worked so hard at being unpredictable."

Daria's arms pulled forward, tightening into each other.

"What do you mean?" she asked.

"I'm just saying that sometimes it seems as if it makes you as uncomfortable as you want it to make others."

Daria stood up, rubbing her arms. "You know, we've both got work in the morning."

Henry nodded. Daria went into the houseboat to get her things, and then walked back out onto the deck, her hands in her coat pockets.

There was a small splash in the water.

"What do you think that was?" Henry asked.

"Just a rock," Daria said. "See you, Henry."

"Good night, Daria. Good luck with the wheel tomorrow." When she turned around at the end of the dock to look back at him he was still in his chair, legs stretched out toward the water.

Daria slammed the ball of clay down onto the batter board, kicking the flywheel with her foot to start its motion. She wet her hands and cupped them around the slightly flattened ball, centering it, pulling the clay up into a column, then pushing it down into a mound, repeating the motion, a dialogue between hands and clay, feeling for imperfections, flexibility, like the first conversations at a cocktail party. If you paid attention, you could tell if something was going to work or not, before you put a lot of work into it.

It was cold in the studio — a hazard of her occupation. Marion always said that Daria worked in a morgue, but a heated studio would dry out the clay faster, and it was easier to wear big old sweaters and have a hot pot ready for tea. Daria liked to joke that cold studios were why potters so often made mugs; they needed boiling liquids for warmth. Daria huddled into her sweater, waiting for the physical activity to warm her. The studio had the bite of November, the air heavy with moisture. A good day to make pots, but it would take longer for them to dry out.

With her thumb, she drilled a hole in the center of the clay, pressing down on the floor of the mound with the pad of her fingers, widening the opening. Elbows braced tight against her sides for stability, she placed one hand inside, the other cupping the outside, fingers down, thumbs touching each other at the top as she pulled the sides up, making a cylinder, the tips of her fingers creating ridges that moved up the piece as she raised her hands, pulling the clay with her, feeling it follow her lead. She wet her hands slightly and repeated the motion, more slowly this time, the wheel losing momentum, slowing with her. A lot of potters preferred motorized wheels; they were less work, certainly, easier on the knees. But Daria liked the manual wheel — the first, hard kicks, the way the motion smoothed out and followed the natural order of the process, a connection between feet, hands, and center.

There was a knock at the door, startling Daria. No one came to the studio; even Marion knew better than to come to any door but her apartment.

She cleaned off her hands with a rag and opened the door to find an oblong shape wrapped in a white cloth, laid on the tiles of her doorstep. She picked it up and felt the warmth coming through the material: she smelled the thick, golden scent of freshly baked bread as she unwrapped the loaf. She pulled off a chunk and bit into it, feeling the crunch of the crust against her teeth, the softness beneath it, the heat rising up into her face.

Tucked into the paper wrapping was a

note. It read: "7 pm tonight. Be hungry."

Utterly predictable, Daria thought. But she smiled.

Henry refused to tell Daria where they were going. The building they ended up at was made of brick and wrought iron, set in the oldest part of town. The neighborhood was once the hub of the city, a patch of land where first settlers and then shopkeepers staked their claims, back when Seattle was the last stop before Alaska, when you could make more money outfitting prospectors than you could ever dig out of the ground or sift from a river. The staid and the desperate and the adventurous mixed together, holding on at the edge of the continent. Nowadays the prospectors were inside the buildings playing with computers, the panhandlers sifting a different kind of river. When Daria was in her twenties and first arrived in Seattle, she had loved the edginess of it all, but it had been a while since she had come down at night and things had become darker somehow. She pulled her coat a little closer and concentrated on the white Christmas lights hung among the branches of the trees lining the street.

Henry looked at her and smiled slightly, opening a door that was almost hidden on the side of the building. They entered an industrial kitchen, its entryway lined with gray plastic garbage cans marked "wheat" and "white." Daria watched as Henry moved confidently through the space, lifting a cloth cover from a large metal pan and inhaling with satisfaction. He wore a long black coat and a scarf wrapped casually around his neck. The whole scene seemed hopelessly, deliciously Parisian, and Daria felt her shoulders relax.

"Is this your bakery?" she asked.

"From five until eleven five mornings a week. Come on," he said, leading her out to a hallway behind the bakery and up a flight of creaking wooden stairs covered with a faded rose-colored runner that smelled of bread and old tobacco. The opaque glass door at the top had an ornate doorbell, and Henry pushed it and waited, until the door opened to reveal a tall, round man in his thirties wearing cargo pants and a tuxedo jacket.

"Henry!" he said joyfully. "The man who makes the world smell wonderful in the morning. I'm glad you're here. And this?" He motioned to Daria.

"I'm Daria," she answered, putting out her hand.

"Beautiful name. Lovely face. I'm William

— welcome to the Underground Restaurant."

"The what?" Daria asked Henry in an undertone.

"You'll see," he whispered.

The space was vast and open, with eighteen-foot ceilings and huge, multipane windows spanning the main wall, looking out to the cranes and containers of the port, the water beyond. The floors were oak, as old as the building itself. In the far corner was a kitchen with a six-burner commercial range and a capacious refrigerator. A wood-fired pizza oven nestled next to the stove, crackling cheerily. A steep red ladder led up to a loft area above the kitchen. The rest of the room was given over to two long tables and a series of ancient couches and over-sized chairs where people were already lounging, wineglasses in hand.

Henry grabbed two wineglasses from the table near the front door and pulled a bottle of red wine from his coat pocket.

"I love the pockets of this coat," he said cheerfully. "You could keep a tuba in them."

The wine was soft and round in her mouth and tasted of cherries and chocolate. The room was warm for all that it was cavernous. Henry and Daria found a pair of chairs and sank in, watching the people around them.

"So, does William live here?" Daria asked.

"Yeah; I met him because he's always the first customer at the bakery in the morning, and he insists on meeting all the new bakers. He owns the building."

Daria looked over at William, at his whirlwind of uncut hair, the frayed edges of his cargo pants.

"Software," Henry explained. "Retired."

"So, is he a chef now?"

"No; that's the chef." Henry pointed to a small, thin man pacing the kitchen area. Henry named a restaurant that Daria had only read about in magazines, a place with eight tables and two seatings per night, no menus. "He works there, but he likes to experiment on his nights off, so William convinced him to do a dinner here. This is the first time it's been at William's loft; the idea is his baby, but it's almost never in the same place twice. Right before I moved here they had an evening in an old warehouse that was going to be torn down. They invited poets and wrote on the walls and ate everything with their hands."

Daria looked over at Henry appraisingly. "Really?"

"I mean, sure, why not?"

William held up a small brass cowbell and

its mellow clang summoned the group to the tables.

It was almost midnight. The tables were cluttered with napkins and used silverware, tablecloths rumpled like bedsheets. The diners reclined in their chairs, hands drifting leisurely back and forth between espresso cups and the last sips of port. Tips of fingers caressed the surface of white plates, snaring the last flakes of chocolate left from cinnamon-dusted truffles. Smells lingered in the air, sliding across bare shoulders, nestling into the curls of hair — risotto and chanterelle mushrooms, sweet and rich and buttery, the bite of Parmesan, the rosemary and white wine and garlic of a slow-cooked pork roast. And bread, of course, the long loaves having been passed hand to hand, chunks pulled off, dipped in small white dishes of green olive oil with dark, molten drops of balsamic vinegar floating in its midst. Wine bottles had long ago lost their ownership, traveling up and down the tables like porters on a train. Artists had met book dealers had met plumbers had met research scientists, people getting up between courses and changing places. Over in the corner, a couple was forming, their heads bending slowly toward each other like candles melting.

Henry was sitting next to Daria on the couch, their shoulders barely touching.

"So, is this how you live?" Daria asked lightly, her hand motioning out across the room, encompassing the scene before them.

"Whenever I can."

Henry paused, looking over at Daria. "I wasn't always that way. I remember being really scared when I started traveling. I acted like it was no big deal, but I was terrified."

"So what happened?"

"I was in Venice one time; I'd been traveling for about five months at that point. It was late November and I got there after dark; it was kind of like here, all foggy and freezing. I remember the cold of the stones coming right up through the soles of my shoes. There was nobody outside, just this strange music that seemed to be coming from everywhere. And then the doors of the churches opened and people came flooding out, all dressed in black. They were all going in the same direction and I just got dragged in with them. I had no idea what was going to happen.

"Finally, we got to the Grand Canal and I saw the church of Santa Maria della Salute on the other side, all lit up. The crowd went across the bridge in front of us — and when I was right in the middle I looked back up the canal and I saw the bridge we should have been on, the last one before the Grand Canal opens up to the lagoon. The bridge I was on wasn't supposed to be there."

"What do you mean?"

"Somebody told me later that the city has a Plague Festival and every year they build a bridge across the canal that goes to Santa Maria della Salute. Then a couple days later, they take it down."

Henry smiled. "I walked across a bridge that doesn't exist. And after that, being scared just didn't seem so important anymore."

Daria looked at him and returned his smile, slowly.

"I like that story," she said.

As they had been talking, people had started reluctantly putting on their coats, silky linings running over skin, spices mixing with perfumes, traveling out into the night.

"Are you tired?" Henry asked. "There's something I'd like to do."

The old inclination for banter, for flirtation rose up in her and then sighed back. Maybe it was the wine, or the hour, but she didn't want the bob and weave of spicy conversation. She just wanted to hear what Henry wanted to do, to say.

"Okay," she replied.

Henry's houseboat was warm, the lights soft.

Daria took off her coat and hung it on the hook by the door. "I thought houseboats were always cold. The water and all that."

"Occupational hazard," Henry replied, and headed for the kitchen. "Come on in here."

Daria watched as Henry filled a battered teapot with water and put it on the stove. Then, out of the refrigerator he took a white plastic container and took off the lid, inhaling with satisfaction.

"Here, smell," he said, holding it out to her. Daria bent her face toward the container, the world disappearing into a tunnel of white walls and the oatmeal-colored mass rising up toward her, bubbling slightly. She inhaled; the scent was complicated, elusive, a cross-weave of sweet and sharp, sand and sea and sun. It reminded her of the Amish guilt-bread starter, but something was different.

"What is it?"

"Sourdough starter. A friend gave me this

one — it's over one hundred years old." Henry's voice held more than a touch of pride.

"How?"

"You feed it."

"Like a pet." Daria's expression was amused.

"You know, a hundred years ago, this starter kept someone alive." Henry's tone was firm, educational. "All it took was this and flour and water and salt and you had food. There are legends about gold miners in Alaska sleeping with their starters at night to keep them from freezing, and pioneer women passing them down for generations. But you know the coolest thing?"

Daria marveled at the way Henry's voice accelerated with excitement. How was it, Daria wondered, that anybody could be so thrilled about yeast at one in the morning?

"The starter attracts the wild bacteria that's floating in the air around it — and the bacteria are different depending on where you are. So if you breathe in, you are smelling all the places it's been."

Daria took the container back, bent over it once again. It was so different from clay — cool, yes, with that same slightly sharp, slightly metallic undertone, but while clay smelled quiet, the starter was a flurry of activity. Where had it traveled? she wondered. What part of the smell had come from here, where Henry lived?

Henry clicked on the oven controls and turned to Daria.

"Want to make bread?" he asked.

The dough was rising in a ceramic bowl, set near the oven for warmth. Daria had watched as Henry poured dry yeast into warm water, added some honey, and swirled it all together, the yeast melting into soft brown clouds that foamed and bubbled. He added the sourdough starter and cup after cup of flour, a bit of salt.

"I like to play with the old recipes a bit," he said with a grin. "Now it needs a chance to rise." He poured hot water into two cups, added chamomile tea bags and handed one mug to Daria, carrying his to the living room. Daria followed him.

"I love this part," Henry said as he settled into the couch. "You can smell it all growing. It's different than when it's baking. I like that, too, but there's something about this part. Maybe it's that you have to wait; I don't know."

Daria took off her shoes and sat sideways across from Henry, her head turned slightly, looking out at the water. She didn't even know what time it was anymore. Henry took one of her feet and pulled it to him, rubbing his thumb along the instep in time with the slight rocking of the water below them.

"I love houseboats," he said. "They remind me of my grandfather's fishing camp. My family went there every once in a while. I would take a rowboat out to the middle of the lake and pretend I was fishing, but I would just sleep. I loved the way the water moved under the boat."

"Hmm . . ." Daria could feel Henry's thumb working along the curves of her right foot.

"So, what is it about octopus pots?" Henry asked.

Daria's head rested on the back of the couch. "When I was about six," she said finally, "my dad took me to this museum. There was an exhibit of Greek artifacts, and they had this ancient octopus pot. I didn't know what it was; I was a kid — it looked like a place to put your secrets. It was terracotta, this amazing, warm orange. The base was so prim and fragile-looking, and then it just curved out, and closed in again. I wanted to put my hands on it so badly. When I started working with clay, it's all I ever wanted to make."

She raised her head. "My mom always

wonders why I don't make something more practical. It doesn't even matter to her that I make a living at this."

"Well, she has a point." Henry gazed across at her, his face serious. "I can barely remember the last time I caught an octopus."

Daria shot a look at him and saw the lift at the corner of his mouth.

Her eyes grew wide and she let loose a deep, full-throated laugh. "You know," she said after a while, "I just never thought of it that way."

The room got quiet. The air was changing, the smell filtering out from the kitchen. Henry's hands were warm on Daria's foot and she closed her eyes, breathing in. When she spoke again, her voice was lower.

"You know, when my dad took me to that museum — we went because, back when I was about five years old, my mom started kicking me and my dad out of the house every Sunday. She said she wanted to make bread and we'd be in the way.

"So Dad and I would go to the museum, or a park, or a movie. I loved spending time with him. And at the end of the day we'd go home, and the house would smell like bread and Mom would just be all lit up. She'd even let me have a slice of bread, before dinner and everything. And each time I'd think, That's it, she's happy. She's going to stay that way.

"But by the next morning, she'd be all tight and angry and nothing I did was right. I remember wondering why she didn't just kick me out every day and make bread. Dad finally gave up and left but Mom wouldn't let him take me with him. I don't know why not."

"When was the last time you saw her?"

"I came out here to visit Marion after I graduated from college and I stayed. I went back once, for my grandmother's funeral a couple years ago."

"Do you miss her?" Henry asked.

"Who?"

"Your mom."

Daria just looked at him.

Henry checked his watch. It was still dark outside, the houseboat redolent with the smell of yeast.

"Time to work the dough," Henry said.

In the kitchen, Henry tipped the bowl, loosening the dough from the sides with a thin curve of plastic and letting it fall onto a thin slab of marble where it lay, quivering, an inflated mass with the texture and color of cold porridge.

Daria looked at the dough skeptically. She had been expecting soft, white, fluffy — the baby's bottom everybody always talked about when they went rhapsodic over making bread. This dough looked distinctly like a papier-mâché project gone bad.

"Doesn't it need something?" she asked tentatively.

"It's fine. Just slip your fingers in from the sides."

The second she touched the dough it seemed to latch on to her skin, clinging to her hands, greedy and thick, webbing her fingers. She tried to pull back, but the dough came with her, stretching off the counter, as unyielding as chewing gum. Clay was nothing like this.

"Something is wrong. Shouldn't we add some flour or something?"

"It's fine." Henry was unconcerned. "Just pick it up so it stretches."

The dough hung down from her fingers, elongating, grotesque, like a cat dangled by its forelegs.

Bits of dough were working their way up toward her sleeves. In frustration, Daria yanked her right hand out of the mass and used her hip to push her sleeve up. Henry caught sight of the tattoos spiraling their way up her forearm.

Daria looked at him, eyebrows raised. She was used to this moment, although reactions took different forms. The prurient curiosity, the instant come-ons, the self-congratulatory open-mindedness.

Henry smiled, pushed up the short sleeve of his T-shirt to reveal his shoulder.

"Solomon Islands," he said, nodding toward an intricate black design. He pointed to his other shoulder. "Texas."

"Well, okay then," she said, and smiled. She looked down at her hands. "You know, this is a mess."

"It's fine. Give it a slap on the counter."

"What?"

"Slap it on the counter."

Daria let the dough droop onto the marble surface.

"That was ridiculous. Give it a good thwack."

Daria looked up at Henry. "Really?"

"It's okay; you won't hurt it."

Daria slid her hands back under the sides of the dough again and raised it off the marble, letting it stretch. Then she raised it higher, slapping the end against the counter like a wet towel. The sound was loud and solid.

"Good," said Henry. "Now fold it over and just keep doing that."

Daria hit the dough against the counter with a firm smack. Fold. Smack. Fold. She could feel the dough changing under her hands, becoming more elastic. Still it seemed a far cry from the dough she had expected; she couldn't be doing it right.

"Are you sure we shouldn't add flour or something?"

"It's fine; it's almost there." Henry's voice was unconcerned. "See how you are getting the air in, the way the strands of gluten are forming? It's lovely."

Daria pulled her hands out of the dough and stood to the side. "Your turn."

Daria watched as Henry nodded and stepped forward, cupping his hands gently around the irregular shape. He stretched it up and folded it over, his movements casual, affectionate — back and forth, back and forth — an interplay of dough, hands, air. With each repetition, the dough began to cling more to itself, less to the counter. And then, as she watched, the rough texture smoothed out, the dough became smooth and white, extending and springing back in his grasp.

"That's incredible," she said.

"A French guy taught me. I had never realized before how alive this stuff is. It's like a puppy." He grinned.

"Now," he said, "we form the loaves."

Henry cut the dough in half. As she watched, he folded in the edges of one of the portions, one over the other, rounding the dough using the open palms of his hands. Daria watched, mesmerized by the way the dough seemed to relax as his hands moved across it, take the shape he was offering.

"Your turn," he said.

Daria washed the old dough from her hands and toweled them dry. Stepping over to the counter, she brought her clean palms to the surface of the dough. It was soft, expectant; she could almost sense the air moving through it. She closed her eyes and remembered what she had seen Henry do, relaxing her hands into loose parentheses, sliding them gently over the dough, shaping it, feeling it warm as skin beneath her hands.

She opened her eyes and gazed at the round loaf in front of her, then at Henry.

"Look at that," she said, and she reached up for the kiss that was waiting in his smile.

Daria lay next to Henry in his bed, inhaling the smell of baking bread that filled the house, the man beside her. Warm sugar, fields in the summer, the slight sharpness of wine. She wondered if anyone had ever made a perfume that was the essence of bread, but even then, how could you get it to cover one person so evenly, to sink into hair, hands, the warm expanse of a chest?

But it was in her, too, she realized, holding her wrist up to her nose. She burrowed in closer to Henry and inhaled the scent at the base of his neck.

"How are you?" he asked.

"Happy," she said.

"Bread does that to people," he commented with a grin.

Daria's legs straddled the potter's wheel, her hands cradling the mound of clay set at its center. Outside it was raining lightly, the drops falling in harpsichord notes down the gutters, running out to the kitchen garden, tilled under for the winter. The CD that Henry had given her whirled in the old, beat-up CD player on the counter and she heard a woman's voice singing, almost a man's, deep and low, like gravel on a dirt road. At some point the line between music and emotion was ground away and it rolled out, unrestrained — the joy of a child, the mourning of a widow, the anger of man in a world where only the exit doors opened.

Daria kicked the wheel and felt the clay moving between her wet palms. She worked the mound, raising it up, pushing it down, feeling its flexibility, the solidity. She opened the base with her thumb, and then started to pull the shape up and out, into a bowl.

A Sunday in January, the cold air pushing against the windows, hanging low and foggy over the water outside Henry's houseboat. Daria pulled two loaves from the oven, reveling in the warmth of the kitchen and the heat that came through the hot pads in her hands. The tops of the bread were brown, full and mounded.

Over the past few months she had become more adept at making bread, although the seagulls had been well fed on her first attempts. But she loved weekends now, the wonderful merry-go-round of kitchen and bed as the bread evolved through its stages — her favorite part when the dough went into the oven and she and Henry would lie in bed in the loft, her head on his shoulder while he told her tales of kind strangers and daring adventures, stories of his travels filling the houseboat along with the smell of baking bread.

"Can we go sometime?" she would ask him. And they would talk of places they would go, people they would meet, their words enfolding her like blankets.

Somehow Henry always managed to finish a story just as the bread was ready in the oven. Today's loaves were perfect, Daria thought, looking at them; she finally had it right. She heard the phone ring and Henry talking softly in the loft.

"That was Marion," Henry said as he came down the ladder into the kitchen. "She called looking for you. Your mom is in town and Marion wanted to know if we would come to dinner. I said yes." He said it casually, like a robber explaining that he had simply confused the bank vault with the men's room.

Daria's spine went tight. "What?"

"I think it's a good idea."

"You don't answer for me." She picked up the loaf of bread. The texture was firm, the color evenly brown. She went outside.

She pitched the loaf on the deck and the seagulls moved in, screaming ecstatically.

Henry came up behind her. "Maybe it's time to give her a try," he said.

"You don't know," she said, her voice hard. "You travel — you meet people. Then you leave. They don't follow you around for your whole life, stuck to you. You don't have to see them again."

"Because *you've* seen your mother so recently." Henry's voice flashed cold. He stopped. "I'm sorry." He went back into the house.

When Daria came back in, Henry was cutting a slice from the second loaf, his back to her. He spread butter across its surface and handed the slice behind him without looking. Daria took it, feeling the warmth in her hand.

"I figured you weren't ready for honey on that yet," he said.

"I'm sorry," she said. "This is why I don't want to go. This is what I turn into."

"I'll be there."

"You aren't going to like who you see."

"Her or you?"

"Both."

"Then I'll just pretend I'm meeting someone new, and I'll travel home to Daria."

They had decided to walk to Marion's — Henry said it would be good for them — and the night was clear and cold. Daria wore the scarf Henry had given her for Christmas, wrapped three times around her neck.

"You're disappearing in there," Henry commented.

"If only," she said, listening to the sound of her boots against the cold pavement. He took her gloved hand and put it in his pocket.

By the time they reached Marion's house a couple miles away, Daria's lungs and face felt swept clean. They ran up the stairs and rang the bell, stomping their feet.

Daria's mother answered the door. She looked first at the couple, then beyond to the empty street.

"You walked?" she said. "Isn't it awfully cold?"

Marion had cooked a pot roast and mashed potatoes, something Daria hadn't seen on Marion's table since her husband Terry's cholesterol had spiked. Henry and Daria had brought a loaf of bread that had been warmed up in the oven after its cold journey. The basket was making its last rounds of the table, Terry happily using the crust to wipe up the last of the pot roast juice.

"Henry," said Daria's mother, "Marion tells me you're a baker." On the other side of the table, Daria stiffened slightly and reached for her wineglass.

"I hear we have that in common," Henry commented.

"We do?"

"Well, I've been hearing stories about your bread-making days, when Daria was younger."

Daria's mother shook her head slightly. "Oh."

"So you must have loved bread," Henry continued, nodding encouragement.

"I suppose." She passed the basket and stood up from the table. "I'm just going to check out the back porch."

As she left the room, Daria turned to Marion. "She hasn't quit?"

"No." Marion glanced over at her husband. "And it's driving Terry crazy."

"And what's with not liking bread? It was practically her religion."

Marion looked puzzled. "Really? I don't remember that. She must have started after I left." Marion paused, reaching back in her mind. "I remember her painting, though."

"Painting?" Daria put down her fork.

"Yeah, she had this studio; she was always in there. When I was little, she'd forget to take me to school sometimes."

"What studio?"

"Oh." Marion stopped, her expression changed. "That's right — you wouldn't have seen it. That was your room."

"How could you not tell me that?"

"I don't know; I'm sorry. I suppose by the time you were old enough, everybody had forgotten about it."

116

■ ■ ■ ■

Daria's mother was on the back porch, wrapped in an old sweater of Terry's, lighting a cigarette. Daria smelled the air, figured it was the second one. She stood in the door frame for a moment, then stepped out and closed the door.

"Tell me what I did."

"Daria, you sound like a teenager." Her mother, of course, was right.

Daria shifted her feet across the planks of the porch floor.

"Tell me what I did. It's been like this for as long as I can remember, and I don't know why."

Behind the glass door, Marion walked by, plates in her hand. She paused; Terry walked up behind her and gave her a small push in the direction of the kitchen.

"It doesn't really have anything to do with you, Daria."

"How can you say that?"

"You were just what happened." Daria's mother knocked her cigarette on the side of the railing and watched the ash fall down into the grass. Daria waited.

"Your father had been out of work for a couple of years," her mother said. "You wouldn't remember; he never wanted you to know about all that. Back then, though, it was all he could think about. But that night . . .

"Anyway. It was my fault. The least I could do was grow up and act like a real mother."

"So you gave up painting?" Daria tried to imagine what it would be like not to touch clay, not to walk into the quiet, untouched space of her studio in the morning, not to have designs and shapes and textures to play with in her head. "That must have been awful."

"It was."

"And you couldn't have children and paint, too?"

"That was the deal."

"Dad said that?"

"No. He wouldn't have. It was my deal."

"Mom." Daria stepped closer.

"So now maybe you see" — Daria's mother turned to her, her tone light and conversational — "why I wish you did real art."

Daria and Henry sat on the bus, riding home. Marion had offered them a ride, but Daria said no. At the next stop, a father and his young daughter got on; the daughter had a stuffed toy monkey in her hand, all long legs and dangling arms. She was talking to her father as they got on the bus — about the height of the steps, the quarters in her hand, how dark it was, how maybe they would see fairies out the window if the fairies didn't think anyone was watching.

Daria watched the two as they found seats and sat down. The little girl was talking happily, the flow of her words bright and shiny, like candy falling from a piñata. But what struck Daria was the expression on the man's face as he looked at his daughter, the way the love seemed liquid, pouring over the girl next to him.

"Look," she said to Henry, and pointed.

Henry smiled. "That's a beautiful thing."

"My mother will never look at me like that. Never."

Henry gazed at her for a moment. "Maybe not," he said quietly.

She looked back at him.

"So," she said, finally. "What are we going to do now?"

"Why don't you tell me a story?" he said. "Your turn."

Daria paused, thinking. It had started to rain and the black pavement shone in the streetlights. The bus growled as it changed gears and continued on its route; three rows up, the little girl had quieted as she gazed out the window.

"Once upon a time," Daria began, "my sister made a chocolate cake, three layers tall . . ."

SARA

When Sara was a little girl, one of her favorite activities had been to go to the airport with her twin brother, Henry, and their mother to pick up friends and family who were flying in to visit. Sara loved arriving at the airport early so they could go to the gate and choose the hard plastic chairs with the best view of the deplaning passengers. She would sit, her shoes discarded below her, the toes of her outstretched feet swinging above the floor, and watch what she and Henry called the animal parade. There were the bird-passengers, all floating scarves and barely restrained carry-on bags, flying down the long ramp into the arms of loved ones; the timid and hopeful, scanning the crowd like long-necked giraffes for someone who might or might not be there; the polar bears who looked neither right nor left as they waded back into the sea of their lives. Sitting in their chairs, Sara and

Henry played a game; out of the parade, they chose the one they called the dolphin — the person with a face full of assurance or curiosity, who moved as if the world was water meant to swim in. The air always seemed different around those people, a bit of electricity slipped in among the oxygen molecules. One time it was a young woman, a camera slung over her shoulder, her clothes beaten with miles, a smile on her open, suntanned face.

Back then, people were always asking Sara what she wanted to be when she grew up. She never knew what to tell them. But at the airport that day, Sara had decided that what she really wanted to be was the woman getting off the plane.

In elementary school, Sara had learned to see the year as divided into two parts. There was school, when she and Henry and their father packed their lunches every day and set out — Sara and Henry to learn whatever was thrown in their direction, their father to teach physics at the high school. After the school day was over, their mother cooked while Sara and Henry did homework and their father created lesson plans swiftly and efficiently. In the evenings after he finished his work, their father would pull out huge

pads of paper that he filled with designs —
cogs and wheels and handlebars, sails and
pontoons and streamers.

Then there was summer, when their father
set aside the grading pen and the papers
and the books and dove into the garage like
the first kid in the pool on Memorial Day.
Their father would cut and weld, the noise
caterwauling through the neighborhood,
and over the weeks, the drawings that Sara
and Henry had peeked at when they thought
their father wasn't looking turned into
mechanical creations, long-legged contraptions with giant wheels, or dainty little crafts
with sleek metal flanks and neon-colored
wings.

Toward the end of each August, their
father would pack up that summer's creation in a trailer that he attached to their
station wagon and set off, to return a few
days or a week later, sunburned and joyful,
his creation usually dented and missing a
few pieces.

When they were young, Henry and Sara
had stayed home with their mother during
their father's summer excursions. Their
mother would occasionally question their
father about his use of time, remarking that
there were other, perhaps more important
concerns, such as patching the roof before

the winter rains.

Their father would just smile and say, "Remember the motto of the race, Lyla." And he would make Sara and Henry pancakes, as small as quarters, that they stacked into towers so they could watch the syrup dripping down from one to the next.

Spying on their father's garage activities had been a summertime game for Sara and Henry when they were young. They would pull crates across the yard and peer through dusty windows, volunteer to take their father glasses of lemonade, reporting back to each other about what they saw, until the summer they were eight and their father turned to them casually at breakfast one morning and said, "Want to help me today?"

They had gone in the garage before, of course, but never as members of the team; the very air felt different. Sara had found herself wishing there was a uniform she could put on, a hat she had to wear. Maybe they could make badges, she thought, but looking at Henry's and her father's faces, already intent upon the bits and pieces of metal on the table, she rapidly discarded the thought for the reality.

There was, as their father explained, plenty of physics involved; they were building an entry for a kinetic sculpture race, with the emphasis on every one of the words. Each human-powered machine competed not only for the aesthetics of its design and decoration — "aesthetics" in this case applied in the loosest and most creative of fashions — but for its durability and speed in a course that included road, water, mud and sand. And while finishing was not necessarily required for an entry to be considered successful, the race was not nearly as much fun if you sank, her father noted.

There was much to be learned about balance and weight and momentum. It made Sara think about her own body, which seemed to be constantly stretching and growing and shifting, feet becoming bigger, legs longer, each change requiring an equivalent internal adjustment. Some designs needed triangulation for support, her father explained, which made them sturdier but slowed them down. Too slim a design, however, and you couldn't float in water. Mud, well, that was almost impossible, their father told them; mostly what you needed for mud was patience.

Sara, who had inherited a bit of her mother's practicality, commented early on that a solitary human being, without the trappings of metal and wood, giant fake flowers or papier-mâché animal heads, would perhaps be the most efficient entry of all.

"Well, yes," her father commented, smiling, "but what would be the fun in that?"

Sara and Henry had begged to go to the kinetic sculpture race with their father that first garage summer. Their mother said they were too young, but their father simply replied that she should come along to make sure everything was all right. The four of them set off in the station wagon at the end of August, its back compartment filled with camping gear, pulling the long trailer behind them, traveling up the coast along beaches and into forests.

While they were driving, their mother told them factual tidbits about the places they were passing. Initially she read from a guidebook, but at one gas station the book mysteriously disappeared and after that, as the miles passed and they got farther from home, the stories began to lose their boundaries, meandering into worlds where gnomes and trolls lived in holes at the base of ancient, towering trees, where rain brought more than flowers from the ground. In the evenings they would stop to camp and their father, who never cooked at home, became the chef of nightly feasts prepared over a campfire, sausages dripping fat and making the burning logs spark and sizzle, marshmallows tanned over the embers, smooshed between crisp squares of graham crackers, the heat of the marshmallows softening the chocolate layer below. After dinner, they played cards by lamplight in the tent, Henry stockpiling sevens because he liked the shape of the number, and then they slept all together in the canvas tent, the symphony of their breath mingling with the crackling sounds of small animals moving in the undergrowth below trees dripping with moss.

At the end of the third day they had stopped in an old Victorian seaport, perched on the edge of nowhere, Sara was sure, for the highway simply ended at the edge of town and there was nothing but water at the other side. The brick buildings on the main street seemed frozen in time, tall and stately and ornate. Sara half expected to see carriages come rattling down the street, which would turn to cobblestones under their wheels, and drunken sailors flying out through the old stained-glass barroom doors. It felt like a movie set, a feeling reinforced by the costumes of the people walking down the street, wearing everything from Victorian bustles and top hats to flowing tie-dyed robes in rainbow colors. There was a trio dressed up as the Scarecrow, the Tin Woodsman and the Cowardly Lion; when they spotted Sara they raced toward her, begging her to be their Dorothy, but Sara's father explained she was needed for their own entry, the theme of which he refused to divulge to any of the other contestants before race time the following day.

The morning of Sara and Henry's first race, their father had woken them early, handing them white lab coats. His hair was wild about his head and he had huge, black-framed glasses perched on his nose.

"Okay," he said, "the Mad Scientists are ready to roll."

Sara and Henry grinned at each other, the excitement almost more than they could stand. They helped pull their entry from the trailer, admiring again the long, sleek metal cover overlaying the minimalist brilliance of its multi-seat bicycle frame, the flowing white banners, the whimsical wooden grasshopper legs that Henry had insisted they add. They rolled it to the starting line, surrounded by a giant purple bird, a fanciful carriage drawn by mechanical horses, a bicycle topped with an elegantly sinuous metal hedgehog and a happy yellow bug-eyed airplane.

"This gives eccentric its own meaning," Sara and Henry's mother commented, but Sara could see the smile bubbling under her words. The day before, Sara had caught her parents holding hands when they thought no one was looking.

"Okay, everybody ready?" Tubas burped and clown horns blared. "Okay, but before we go . . ." A drum rolled, badly, and laughter erupted. "What is the motto of the race?" the announcer yelled out. The crowd roared back, the words muddied.

"What did they say?" Sara asked her father. He looked down at her and smiled.

"They said — Adults need to have fun so children will want to grow up."

And so, for the next ten years, Sara and Henry's summers had been filled with screwdrivers and wrenches and bicycle and boat parts, with dreams of flying and floating and racing down hills in cars that looked like butterflies, bicycles that felt like small boats sailing through air.

And for ten winters they waited for the moment when the whole process would start over again, when their father would look up, eyes lit with excitement, and say, "*I have an idea."*

Sara had met her future husband during her freshman year in college when they were assigned as lab partners in an art photography class. Dan had just needed another elective in his schedule, but it was clear to everyone that he had an eye that saw moments more than things, his photographs reaching out to the viewer, making them step closer into the story held on the paper.

Dan always said later that he had had a head start with Sara, getting to spend all that time with her in the darkroom, with its heady mix of chemicals and soft red light. Sara knew better. She had fallen in love with him the moment she saw his hands gently unrolling the developed film from the round metal cylinder, the way his fingers seemed to caress the edges of the ribbon of negatives, the anticipation in his face as he waited to see what had made its way into the camera. Some people said you could know before you looked, but Dan didn't agree. He said half the fun was seeing what you didn't know you'd taken, the story that had found you.

And yet when Dan, despite the urgings of the teacher, had declined to see photography as more than an extracurricular activity and chose instead to stay with the architecture major that would provide a living for Sara and the children they wanted to have, she had stepped under the wing of his practicality with relief. They got married the minute after they graduated.

From the beginning, Sara had felt the pull toward procreation, toward Dan, as strong as the current of a river, deep and sensual, impossible to resist when she was ovulating. During the weeks when she was not fertile, she had felt like paper, thin and insubstantial, ready to blow away with the next wind. Then the current would return and she would slide into it, let go, roll over to Dan and trace the lines of his shoulder blades with the tip of her tongue, let her fingers slide down the muscular lengths of his legs. Dr. Jekyll and Mrs. Hormones, Dan said with a laugh, but he had loved the feeling of the river as much as she did, the way it turned his wife into something fluid and rich and powerful, so absolutely sure of what she wanted. It had taken all the willpower they had to wait to conceive a baby until Dan was through architecture school and they had more than a studio apartment and a beat-up Volkswagen bus.

But when it finally happened, Sara loved being pregnant, the mystery of not knowing who was inside her, her own roll of film waiting to be developed. She and Dan would go to movies and scan the credits for names they liked. Dan would write the top contenders on strips of paper and lay them across Sara's burgeoning stomach — to see if they fit, they would joke. They had spent weekends painting the baby's room, evenings putting together the crib, and Sara had fallen in love with her husband's hands all over again, the way they held a paintbrush or a screwdriver or the small of her back, the seemingly effortless capability of them.

While most women she knew wanted only bland food when they were pregnant, Sara was ravenous for new spices, the taste of heat. Coriander and cumin, habanero peppers, fish oil and red pepper flakes, a hot sauce from New Orleans that had them all sweating. She traveled among the spices, searching out the new and different, her ever-increasing stomach preceding her like a masthead on her ship of discovery. Dan would look across the table at her and smile, although she realized at one point that the lunches he was taking to work were becoming increasingly bland — yogurt and bananas, a bottle of Tums. It was, in a way, a relief to both of them when Tyler was born and the doctor told her to cut back on the spices as they might give Tyler colic. It was easier to slide into the world of white — milk, blankets, clouds.

Caught up as she was in her own internal travels, it hadn't bothered Sara that her twin brother had taken off after college with a backpack and a startlingly small amount of money, a one-way ticket to Asia in hand. Henry's letters had taken forever to get to her, often arriving when he was already in the next country. Word pictures distilled on whispery airmail paper — a faded red temple, standing in the middle of a lake like a ghost; two-thousand-year-old rice terraces, their boundaries irregular and sinuous, cascading their way down a slope; a stone Buddha so large Henry said he could have slept in its outstretched hand; yellow ginkgo leaves against stone steps. Sara saw his life in snapshots, like walking past open doors of hotel rooms and catching an image before the door closed again.

She couldn't write back, Henry already gone by the time she knew where he was. She didn't know what she would have written anyway, how to describe her life, the lush, stationary physicality of motherhood. The only way to understand would be to hold it in your arms.

Sara and Dan's twins had been, quite frankly, a surprise, both their conception and the abundance of it. Tyler had just turned five; Dan was moving steadily up the ladder in the architecture firm. All of a sudden, life was crowded — their house too small, their hands too few.

But after Hillary and Max had been born, she could never have imagined sending them back. Even in the chaos of the move to the new, larger house — the ridiculous timing of it all, the babies too early and barely a week old, the cloth diapers accidentally packed in some box they would find years later when Hillary and Max were entering kindergarten — there had been the excitement of the new and different. She could almost pretend she was traveling.

She wondered sometimes, though, what she would have done without the women who entered her life during that time. Marion, Dan's boss's wife, setting up a baby-holding circle and introducing her to Kate and Caroline and Daria. And then there was Hadley, Sara's next-door neighbor, who had walked across the lawn and into Sara's living room that morning not long after Sara moved in, gently taking one of the babies into her arms when Sara had in her exhaustion completely forgotten she was holding two. The way, after that day, Hadley would often come over at five in the evening — witching hour, they called it — and create a pasta sauce for dinner or entertain a baby, the afternoons she would take Tyler to the bookstore to find a new book, or for a walk around the neighborhood. Hadley felt like family to Sara, someone who knew what she needed without her saying a word. It was, Sara thought, just a bit like having Henry back.

Time went on, life with the children unfolding in its own ecosystem, small plastic toys seeming to grow up from the carpet like mushrooms, clothes falling to the floor like autumn leaves. Every once in a while she would blaze through the house and clean everything — at which point, the process would start all over.

An afternoon came when Max and Hillary were almost one year old, Tyler closing in on six. Sara had finally gotten the twins down for their nap and had been reading to Tyler from *Gulliver's Travels*, while Tyler made stunningly complicated constructions from his Legos on the floor in front of her. Tyler loved *Gulliver's Travels*, the idea of a big, strapping man suddenly overwhelmed by small people, then turning into a small man surrounded by big people. For an imaginative child, the suspension of disbelief required was not a large one, and Tyler often requested that Sara read the book to him, her voice mingling with the sound of the plastic blocks clicking one into another, a musical score to his childhood.

Tyler had gone off to find the plastic cockpit door for his Lego fighter plane, a piece Sara was certain had long ago become food for the vacuum and he was equally sure was floating in his aquarium. Sara sat, thinking about the story. She looked around her, at the plastic figurines and tiny cars and stuffed animals covering her floor, the table with its snack plates still waiting to be cleared, the new puppy sniffing about the chairs in hopes of a forgotten windfall, the pile of travel books she had forgotten she had ever wanted to read.

And she found herself wondering at what point in her life she had ceased to be Gulliver and had become the strings holding him to the ground.

When Sara learned about Kate's diagnosis, it had been like feeling the first tremors of an earthquake, the small, inescapable certainty that the way you viewed the world was changing quite literally under your feet. When Marion suggested that their group shift the focus from holding babies to helping Kate, Sara had quickly agreed, eager to return the favor Kate had so easily given her.

As part of the new circle, Sara would go over to Kate's house for a few hours on the weekends while Dan took care of the kids, and keep Kate company as she fought off the side effects of her chemo sessions. Standing in the kitchen making soup, Sara watched Kate wading into an ocean of chemicals, as if the act of submersion would get her to her daughter on the other side; she watched Kate's daughter's eyes following her mother, the fear in them carefully covered when Kate would turn toward her.

Afterward, Sara would go home and hold her children, as many as she could fit in her lap, as long as they would stay. She would breathe in the sweet-sweat smell of their hair and wish she and her children and Dan could all simply melt into one, indivisible whole. But at the same time — and this was inexplicable to Sara — there was a part of her that was more restless than she had ever been.

Sara didn't know how Kate had guessed what she was feeling. But that evening of Kate's victory celebration, Kate had looked across the table with such compassion and more than a little bit of mischief and given Sara the challenge of taking a trip alone, as if, fully aware of the consequences, she was handing a child a chocolate éclair before breakfast.

Sara had quickly buried the idea at the bottom of her to-do list, applying a natural rank-ordering that put real-world deadlines at the top — restocking her supply of boxed macaroni and cheese, scheduling the twins' first dental appointments, making the plane reservations for Dan's conference in New York. It sat there, a small, stark word — "travel" — as if it was something you could check off at the end of a day, an hour's effort, like picking up milk at the grocery store. Most days, she didn't scan all the way down the list; the only way to keep moving was to concentrate on the priority items. But when she did, she could see it sitting there, more or less patiently, like a present or a bomb, waiting to be unwrapped.

■ ■ ■ ■

Two months later, Henry came into town just in time for Thanksgiving, bringing with him the smells of travel, cigarette smoke from a crowded train in Poland, yeast from a bakery in Alsace-Lorraine. The toys he brought the children were not made of plastic; the music he hummed was nothing she recognized. He was her twin, and looking at him she had never felt more as if he was her second half, the one she had sent out into the world while she stayed home. She felt as if she could not stand close enough to him, listen to his stories long enough, as if doing so would make her a complete person again.

One morning, Henry saw her to-do list on the kitchen counter and whistled at its length, the sound drawing in and stopping when he reached the bottom of the list.

"Travel?" he asked.

Sara told him about Kate's challenge.

"Where are you going?" Henry was excited. "When?"

Sara mentioned the kids, Dan, the house. Henry listened, letting the list unfurl in front of her like a red carpet leading to nowhere. He nodded, saying nothing, but after that, Sara noticed that he became more lax about keeping his things in the guest room — a photograph of a statuesque white castle finding its way onto the living room table, a package of Swiss chocolate left on the kitchen counter, a heavy flannel shirt smelling of Irish peat fires hung in the hall closet, the smell infiltrating her coat next to it, coming with her as she drove to Tyler's school or walked the dog in the park.

When Henry told her he had found a job at a bakery and a houseboat to live in, she rejoiced. She loved having him stay with them, his easy way with the kids, the conversations she and Henry and Dan would have at night after the kids were asleep. Henry would tell them stories about a winter festival in Germany, the smell of turmeric and hot chili peppers in a port town in Tunisia. Even though he had been with them for almost a month, she still felt greedy for his presence and was glad he would be living nearby. The world simply felt bigger when he was there.

Introducing Henry to Daria was simple. From the moment she had heard Kate assign Daria the challenge of making bread, Sara saw the potential for matchmaking — and then Henry had come home, as if he had heard the plan that was forming in her head. After Henry met Daria, he accused Sara of trying to make him settle down and stay in the Northwest forever, but he smiled as he said it.

Henry didn't give up on his quest to make Sara travel, even after he moved out of their house. When he called, he would leave messages in various languages — Spanish, French, Italian, Chinese, forcing her to look up translations, listen to the sound of new rhythms and intonations. He and Daria went on a quest to convince the twins to eat a wider variety of foods, bringing in spices that Sara hadn't used since she was pregnant with Tyler. The children were surprisingly excited by the foods, although it may have had as much to do with the costumes that Henry and Daria would wear; the night they cooked Indian food, Daria arrived in a sari, the glow of its green silk set against her pale skin and red hair. The twins stared, awestruck.

One Friday night in January, four months after the evening in Kate's garden, Sara and Dan, Henry and Daria and Hadley all sat around the table in the dining room. Max and Hillary were asleep; Tyler was drawing flying contraptions while lying on the floor in the living room nearby.

"Okay," Henry announced, "who else thinks Sara needs to get off her butt and travel somewhere?"

All hands were raised, except Sara's.

"But what about the kids?" she asked. She could feel panic fingering its way into her throat. Under the guise of reaching for her wineglass, she did a quick head check for Tyler, listened with one ear for sounds from the baby monitor sitting on the sideboard.

"Sara." Daria leaned forward. "When was the last time you spent a night away from your kids?"

Sara and Dan shared a quick look.

"Wait," Daria said incredulously. "*Never?* Okay, that's changing right now."

Hadley spoke up, nodding toward Dan. "Sara, we've got it all figured out. Dan can drive Tyler to school; I can take care of the twins during the morning. Henry and Daria will come over after Henry's shift at the bakery and stay until Dan is home again. It's perfect — although you should feel flattered that it takes four of us to do your job."

Sara looked at Dan. He smiled at her. "It's a great idea."

"I agree with Dan." Henry's face had what their mother always called his adamant look. "You need some adventure; it'll wake you up."

"But what about the kids?"

Henry looked over at her and grinned. "Remember the motto of the race, Sara."

"So where shall you go on your travels?" Eleven A.M. the following morning and Henry stood at Sara's back door, a warm loaf of bread in his hands. He was still covered in flour from work — the snow-uncle, Tyler liked to call him — but his determination was clear.

"I don't know," Sara said, letting him into the kitchen. "There are so many choices." While a country checklist for Henry would have relatively few options left, Sara's was wide open. She and Dan had driven three hours to British Columbia for their honey-moon, but you didn't even need a passport in those days, the border guards more like bored attendants at a self-serve gas station.

"Okay, then we play. Travel roulette."

Sara raised an eyebrow.

Henry continued, undeterred. "We find the cheapest flight and that's where you go. Much better than throwing darts at a map. Do you have any idea how much it can cost to get to Tierra del Fuego?"

While Sara made coffee, Henry grabbed Dan's laptop and brought it into the kitchen, cleaning the crumbs and jelly off the table before setting down the computer.

The coffee burbled and the smell of fresh bread filled the kitchen. Sara cut slices of the baguette and put them on a plate with unsalted butter and raspberry jam, the way Henry liked it. She could hear Henry's fingers tapping on the keys, then the table, as he waited for the results of his search.

"All right," he said, as Sara put a mug of coffee in front of him. "We got it. One month from now. Venice or Brazil." He looked up at her. "What do you think?"

"I don't have a passport."

"We'll rush it. Which do you want?"

"Henry, I don't know. This isn't how you make a decision like this."

"I beg to differ; this is exactly how I make a decision like this."

"You. You're used to traveling. You speak languages. You're single."

"You've done twins; you can do anything. Which do you want?"

"I don't know." For Sara, it felt as if a giant curtain hung around her house; anything outside of it was equally foreign.

"Okay, we'll put it up to fate. I know you; you'll want to know where you are staying so you can tell Dan. I'll check with a couple cheap hotels and the first city where we find somewhere for you to stay, that's where you'll go."

Henry's fingers typed rapidly, expertly.

"Have you ever thought of being a travel agent?" Sara asked.

"Hell no. Most travelers are a pain in the ass. Way too jittery." He looked over at her and winked.

They drank their coffee, Sara staring at the back of the computer, waiting. Almost in spite of herself, she could feel excitement rising in her, small and persistent, as if the air around her was suddenly full of laughter.

"Honey," Henry said, looking over at her, "they are on different time zones, and these countries are not known for efficiency. This could take a little while."

They heard the little mechanical bell signaling an inbound email.

"Well, what do you know," Henry said, reading the message. "This great little dive I know has one room available. You are going to Venice."

In the weeks before her trip, Henry was an invaluable source of information — telling her which drugstore would take her passport picture, both ears showing, smiling but without teeth in case she caught the traveling bug and wanted to go places where that might be a sign of aggression. He went through the things in her big suitcase and took out most of them, leaving her with featherweight black clothes that fit in a carry-on, a credit card, and a paperback book for the plane. He took her shopping for comfortable black boots and pitched her tennis shoes back into the closet.

"They'll know you're American," he told her. "But you don't have to advertise."

And he listened as she described her contingency plans over and over — what she'd do if she lost her passport, how Dan and the kids could reach her, how she could always buy clothes if the weather was colder or hotter than she had packed for. He answered questions about Internet cafes and told her how to order coffee, gave her tricks to figure out the exchange rate and get over jet lag.

But one day he simply stopped.

"You're not traveling if you already know everything," he said.

While she understood the concept, it didn't make her comfortable. Home was comfortable. She found herself waiting, almost hoping, for the disaster that would make her unable to leave — a snack assignment for the soccer team, an unforeseen deadline for Dan. She checked the twins hourly for runny noses. Surely they would need her to stay.

The night before her departure, Sara lay in bed next to Dan, watching the numbers on her clock change from one to the next. When she knew Dan was asleep, she took her pillow and slipped out of bed and into Max and Hillary's room. Max had fallen asleep in his new big-kid bed, his back tight against the wall, his stuffed rabbit held in his arms. Hillary was on her stomach, one cheek visible in the glow of the night-light. Sara lay down on the floor between them. If she listened to every breath until she left, she thought, they would all keep breathing until she came back.

And then, even as she was remembering that she hadn't bought an extra box of Cheerios in case they ran out, she found herself on a plane about to head east, the sun setting behind her.

"It's my first time to Europe," she mentioned to the businesswoman sitting next to her. The woman nodded politely, pulled out a pillow and put on an eyeshade. An image of a lioness, regal and bored, came into Sara's mind and she pulled her arm back slightly from the armrest.

Sara sat next to the woman, hearing the plane's engines growl into action, feeling the rumbling movement as they began to taxi down the runway — the way it pushed her spine back in her seat, the opposing pull in the rest of her body, as if she was still holding on to her children's hands, her arms stretching across the growing distance between them.

Stop it, Sara, she told herself. She tried to focus on the luxury of having an entire plane seat to herself, of a carry-on bag that held not a single board book or action figure or diaper. She stared at the flight attendant giving the safety demonstration and after the lecture was over she looked assiduously at the in-flight magazine until the seat belt light turned off. Then she went in the bathroom and sobbed, her face buried in a fistful of rough brown paper towels.

Paris, where she changed planes, was a thunderstorm of languages, none of them hers. She had forty-five minutes to get to her next gate, without the first idea of how to do it. A line stretched down the hall toward an overhead sign that declared "customs." After twenty minutes, a man from India standing behind her explained that she didn't need to wait there.

"You need to go to terminal two," he said, looking over her ticket. "Go to the line for station three."

"Three?" she asked. "For two?"

"Exactly," he answered, nodding matter-of-factly.

But the line for station three led down into the depths of the airport, and as Sara found herself descending deeper, escalator after escalator, caught in a rush of travelers with no option to turn back, she felt her anxiety level rising.

Where was she going? Maybe that man hadn't known what he was talking about, or had sent her in the wrong direction on purpose. She would miss her plane and she didn't know anyone in Paris. How would she get another flight? Could she possibly be failing already at something that should be so easy?

The crowd was going, it appeared, to a line of shuttle buses. With fifteen minutes left before her next flight, Sara looked about her in panic. Which bus? Everyone was moving quickly and purposefully toward vehicles that were rapidly filling. Sara felt the smell of sweat rising off her, the acrid scent of nerves and fear that reminded her of high school dances.

Scanning about her, she spotted a family — mother, father, two teenage children and a grandmother, all dressed in black, speaking a language she hoped was Italian. Sara reached into her jacket pocket and felt Kate's smooth, round beach stone inside. She gripped the rock and blindly followed the family onto a bus as the doors closed behind her.

Oh God, she thought. Please don't let them be going to Spain.

But they *were* Italian, and the teenagers spoke English and they walked her right to the gate and stayed with her until their line for Milan somehow diverged without notice from her line to Venice and she found herself on a plane, breathing hard — until she looked out the window as they soared over mountains that reached up to kiss their wings, and she thought, This is the most beautiful thing I have seen in my life.

She had heard Henry's stories of Venice, about streets made of water and bridges that didn't exist, of tides that could rise and cover the stone streets and piazzas, leaving tourists teetering along the tops of folding tables set up to cross San Marco Square. A city made of islands, buildings resting on what used to be the tops of trees, the forests of Slovenia re-created in the depths of a lagoon, held in place by mud instead of roots, made eternal in an underwater world without seasons.

Even so, she didn't expect it, the way the city opened out in front of her as she left the train and walked through the gates, shifting from *terra* to *acqua* as effortlessly as an amphibian. The way the world changed — cars becoming boats, passengers slipping off their land-selves, laughing and taking pictures. The locals navigated with slick if somewhat grumpy ease through the flurries of tourists, ignoring the ticket booths, striding onto the public water taxis and taking their seats while groups of visiting college students, newlyweds, tired families and retired couples debated which side of the boat would have the better view, who would collect their tickets, how they would know which stop was theirs.

Sara sat among them, watching the light fall sideways onto the thick green water and the faded rose and ivory and terra-cotta facades that lined the canal. Through the huge windows of the elegantly decaying buildings she could just glimpse sculptured ceilings and chandeliers dripping glass; below, the lagoon caressed entry stairs, reaching for doors. The whole vision was so much more theme park than reality that she had to restrain the desire to check to see if the boat was running on rails. Their boat approached the ancient Rialto Bridge and the tourists around her cried out in recognition, raising their cameras like supplicants to capture the vision of the arch, the deeply green wooden doors of the old shops, the cameras aimed down at them. Sara wondered what Dan would photograph if he were here.

Sara counted the exit options carefully, concerned that she might float out into the lagoon and never be seen again, but in the end, her stop was obvious and she navigated her way off the *vaporetto* with only a modicum of bumps and apologies, her carry-on bag bobbling behind her across the metal ramp and the uneven wooden walkway. It was early evening at the tag end of winter, but the city still carried the vibration of movement, people walking purposefully or aimlessly over the bridge and down the stone streets. In the midst of all the people, the postcard stands and pizzerias and alleyways, Sara almost missed the hand-painted sign for her hotel, hanging above an arched, darkened alcove. With a mixed sense of victory and trepidation, she stepped into its gloomy embrace and the world outside diminished. She pushed the doorbell, the tongue of a bronze lion; with a raspy buzz, the door unlatched and she wound her way up the spiraling narrow stairway that rose in front of her.

The front desk clerk greeted her, selecting a key with a bronze fob the size of his palm and taking her down a slim carpeted hallway that sloped disturbingly toward the water. Etchings and posters lined the walls; a series of shelves held books in English, French, German, gifts or castaways, left behind for the next guests. In her jet-lagged state, Sara found herself wondering where the books would go after this. If they liked traveling without knowing where they were going, whom they would meet.

The desk clerk took a corner and pointed down the length of the hallway to the right, to the shared bathroom at its end. Turning to the left, he entered an almost hidden corridor and unlocked a narrow door. Sara could barely make out a twin bed, flush against the wall in the darkened space. A monk's cell. Bypassing the light switch, the clerk walked down the aisle next to the bed and opened the glass window at the far end of the room. Sara heard the muffled sounds of water and boats. Then, with the practiced ease of a professional magician, the man unlatched the heavy wooden shutters and pushed them outward, filling the room with the evening light, the view of a golden palazzo and the white dome of a church beyond. Sara's eyes widened. The clerk accepted her expression as his due and laid the key on the miniature desk next to the window.

"Breakfast will be at eight A.M. We will bring it to your room." He nodded to her and left.

She called her family; after ten minutes of battling with her international calling card, the number went through but by that point Tyler was already on his way to school, Hadley and the twins likely out on a walk. The sound of Tyler's voice on the message made her miss her family with a sharp and sudden longing. All she wanted was to curl up on her single bed and smell the fragrance of her children that still clung to her clothes.

"Enough of that, Sara," she told herself. "You're here; be here." It was what she always said to Tyler when he was frustrated and wanting to be somewhere he wasn't. It made her feel better to say the words aloud, as if perhaps he could hear her.

She washed her face and set off in the direction of a nearby *taverna* she had read about in her bright blue guidebook. After a wrong turn or two and the assistance of a helpful Australian backpacker, she found the restaurant and entered into its warmth, the smell of grilling meat and simmering tomatoes. A waiter approached and she signaled her status apologetically with an upraised index finger; he greeted her, mercifully, with a smile and showed her to a table tucked into a corner.

Sara picked up the menu. She was thinking of ordering pizza; the unrequited call home had left her desiring something familiar. But she remembered that her guidebook had recommended the homemade ravioli, and she found the dish easily enough on the list of offerings that was translated into three languages. An American woman at the next table saw Sara looking over the menu and leaned toward her.

"You know," she said, speaking with the confidentiality and volume of a woman under a hairdryer at a salon, "I almost never go to a restaurant where the menu is written in anything other than Italian — they say those restaurants just aren't authentic — but I had to pee, so here we are."

Sara nodded, smiling politely, but in reality she was grateful for the familiar words on the menu, although even in English she wasn't sure what the sauce for the ravioli was. She was even grateful when the waiter approached, took one look at her and shifted instinctively into English. She pointed to the description of the ravioli on the menu and he smiled knowingly and disappeared into the maze of tables behind him.

She picked up a bread stick and crunched into it, the taste of sea salt and butter surprising her with its delicacy. She took a sip of the mellow red wine the waiter had brought and its warmth soothed her. The world tilted with jet lag, making her feel somehow more above her body than part of it, in this place so utterly unlike her world of plastic Legos and sippy cups.

As she sat at her table, she observed the faces of the other diners — the way their gazes floated over the crowd and then caught at the strangeness of her solitary situation. As a woman alone, she was a source of speculation. She found herself wondering idly what stories people were creating for her, what identities she would make up for herself, trying them on in her mind one after another.

A middle-aged couple came into the restaurant with cameras draped around their necks. As Sara watched, the husband pointed to one of the tables, proclaiming its suitability, and started across the room. The woman paused and then followed him, her words swallowed like the first course of their meal. A few tables away a woman took off her sweater, revealing a backless black dress, wings tattooed across her shoulder blades. Outside, a pair of priests walked by the window, wide-brimmed black hats on their heads, their long dark cassocks fluttering behind them in the chill evening air. Amid the murmurings of the restaurant, Sara could almost hear the creaking of her imagination waking up.

The pasta arrived, four plump squares arranged across her plate, their edges pressed shut in tiny half-moons the size and shape of a child's fingertip. Melted butter flecked with thin, dark shavings flowed languidly over their surfaces and formed a golden pool on the plate around the ravioli. The smell rose up, deep and luxurious, like perfume warmed between the breasts of a beautiful woman.

"*Tartufo*," the waiter said to Sara's inquiring expression. "Truffles."

"Oh my," the American woman at the next table said, and directed her attention to her husband.

Sara took a bite and the taste filled her mouth, dense and rich, like the very essence of longing, then the pasta gave way to warm, fresh ricotta cheese and the sweet earthiness of porcini mushrooms.

"Oh my," said Sara softly to herself.

The light was completely gone from the sky by the time she exited the restaurant but the piazza was lit with the pink glow of the rose-colored streetlamps, the open space still full of people, even though the air was cool. She started back toward the hotel, fully ready to find the bed she had denied herself earlier, her body humming from the meal she had eaten.

As she left the piazza and headed toward the bridge, she heard someone behind her, an inquiring voice. She turned around, wondering if someone was lost. Although she knew she had neither the language nor the knowledge to assist anyone, it made her feel good to think that someone might believe she would be able to help.

A young man with a sweet, open face caught up to her and began speaking in Italian. She shook her head and answered in English that she didn't understand, at which point he switched to a halting version of her own language. He was playing a game, he explained, from the University of Padova — maybe she had heard of it? The university, she said, yes, thinking perhaps this was a scavenger hunt. She remembered them from college, the excitement of the challenges, the joyful embarrassment of asking strangers for things or favors — like a grown-up Halloween, only riskier. She smiled at the memories.

Encouraged, the young man continued. There was a game; he got *punti,* for *baci.*

Baci, she knew. Kisses. She started to pretend not to understand, until she remembered he was speaking mostly in her language and ignorance on her part wouldn't work particularly well. Besides, his face was kind; she sensed none of the signals that usually set her shoulders stiff.

He could kiss her, he explained, on the mouth, or the feet, or on the breast or the armpit. (Was that really what he meant? she wondered. He must have the wrong word — but he was pointing, so it must be.) He seemed a bit embarrassed.

She looked at his face, heard people behind her and realized they were not alone. There was no danger, simply a very odd situation. For heaven's sake, he was a boy and she was a mother.

"On the feet, I guess," she said, half apology, half challenge. "My husband wouldn't like the other options."

He looked truly discouraged, like a child refused a second helping of ice cream. "No, really?"

"Perhaps you should find someone else?" But she said it kindly.

He nodded in lighthearted defeat, leaned in and kissed her cheek, first one, then the other, as if in leave-taking. Then he kissed her quickly, softly on the mouth. It surprised her, the gentleness.

"You won your point," she noted.

"No," he said, "it has to be more . . ." He shrugged his shoulders eloquently.

"Ah, well then," she said, smiling despite herself, and continued on her way, the softness staying on her lips for the rest of her walk like the last taste of dessert. She wondered if she had any idea, really, of what had just happened.

She woke up to the muffled sounds of the first boats moving through the canal outside her window. She lay in bed, the day coming to her in small, liquid moments, sleep slipping into wakefulness like the slow merging of two streams. She reveled in the utter luxury of it, the way the morning lay on her body, golden and full of possibility. For years now, she had woken up like a runner leaping from the starting blocks — her body yanked into consciousness by a baby's wail, the sound of the puppy vomiting, the growl of the trash truck two doors away, their own trash cans still waiting to be put out on the curb. Sleep tossed over her shoulder as she sprinted down the hall, leaving dreams in a scattered trail behind her.

But now she resisted the urge to get up and lay instead in the nest of warmth her body had collected around itself during the night. She let her mind wander, bit by bit, back into her body, the soft edges of dreams blurring her first waking thoughts, the boundaries between sleep and reality am-biguous. She remembered Tyler coming home from school, so excited to tell her about tide pools and the way life thrived in the place between ocean and land. I am in a tide pool, she thought, and smiled.

Then she remembered the present she had found hidden at the bottom of her suitcase, with a note that read: *Open on your first morning in Venice. I love you, Dan.*

It was a camera.

The note inside said: *I thought it was time you had one of these in your hands again. Now, here's a game for you. Go find: a smell, a touch, a taste, a sound.*

There was a knock, and Sara could smell

the soft welcoming scent of coffee even before she opened the door. The clerk brought in a metal tray and with a quick "good morning," he set it on the desk and exited. Sara walked over and inhaled the aroma of freshly baked croissant. She dipped her finger in the small bowl of apricot jam and tasted it, opened the window to an unseasonably warm March morning. Inspired by the view of blue sky and the golden palazzo across the canal, she hopped up on the sill. Out on the canal, a gondolier stood high in the stern of his boat, pushing forward into his pole then pulling it back, an endless give-and-take moving him slowly down the waterway through a parade of early morning water taxis. Sara saw a tourist on a passing vaporetto lift his camera and take a picture of her as she raised her cappuccino to her lips.

How would she find the things on Dan's list? she wondered as she sat on the ledge. It was so like him; they always joked that an architect should think in the box, not outside of it, but that wasn't Dan. As a result, his buildings and houses were elegant and unusual — egoless, one client had said. As if he had simply stepped out of his head and into theirs, seen what they wanted.

Still, how would you capture a smell with

a camera?

Fortified by breakfast, Sara set out, camera in hand. The city seemed to be celebrating the unusual weather; even the dour matrons sweeping their front steps appeared to be doing so in time to music. The last of the schoolchildren raced across the cobblestones in search of a classroom while the sound of church bells rolled across the city, low and round and comforting.

Following the map in her guidebook, Sara crossed the bridge and headed toward San Marco Square, putting the map away when she realized that the route was well marked with yellow signs. She entered a parade of people, surprised at the density. A few businessmen with briefcases moved expertly through the erratic traffic patterns of the tourists, who seemed capable of stopping for any reason — a shop window, a phone call, a bite of pizza. Couples and families gathered for photos on bridges, oblivious to those around them. Groups of teenagers laughed and pushed one another. A couple spoke in loud, flat voices, inveighing against the injustice of both cover and service charges at a nearby restaurant. Gondoliers cast their sales pitches into the crowds, trolling for clients; African men, their skin dark against the white stones and pale visitors, hawked fake Gucci bags. Shopkeepers looked out on it all with bored irritation.

Sara took a quick turn down a side street into sudden, incredible silence.

She was lost. It had taken no more than two turns and she was entirely without bearings. Her guidebook was no help, its maps designed for the broad thoroughfares and direct connections, not the tiny alleyways she found herself in. Forward seemed the best option, so she continued through a low passageway — a tunnel, really, as if someone had simply carved out the first level of a building — and into a bright, open courtyard filled with pigeons. She stopped, unnerved by the sight. Everything held for a moment and then suddenly the pigeons vaulted up into the sky, the sound of their wings deafening. Without thinking, Sara raised her camera to follow their flight. Through the lens she saw an elderly woman standing at a window on the third floor, tossing out bread crumbs. The pigeons circled about her. She looked down at Sara and nodded.

It was funny, Sara thought as she left the courtyard and headed back out into the maze of streets. She couldn't remember the last time she had really looked up and paid attention to anything higher than the top of her children's heads. She had spent the past eight years looking at the ground ahead for things that would trip them, or behind for things they had dropped. The world had diminished to a height of four feet. And yet here it was, with a sky full of birds.

She didn't know how long she had wandered, one street leading to another, each bridge and canal offering views of water and light, each small garden a story hidden behind a gate or wall and visible only from the height of a bridge. As the sun reached higher it pulled the scent out of the canals, thick and complicated, as if seawater could ripen like cheese or wine. She had been warned that in the heat of the summer the smell could be almost overwhelming, but at that moment life still held the balance over decay, barely, poignantly. Sara stood on a bridge and closed her eyes, breathing in. When she opened them she saw a building on the other side of the narrow canal.

The building was sliding into disrepair, the plaster curling back from the worn bricks underneath, green trailing plants growing out from between the cracks and flowing down the walls. The curves of the ancient red roof tiles seemed to be melting into one another; the window shutters hung off their hinges like falling trees. The whole structure was sinking slowly, the straight lines of the window frames bowing into arches as it descended, reaching for the canal below. Sara raised her camera, breathed in and took the picture.

Hours later, without her even knowing how it had happened, the dark and narrow street she was on exited into the broad open field of San Marco Square. Here the crowds had dispersed like wildflower seeds, settling in chairs at the outdoor cafes or sitting on the steps, hands on knees, leaning forward into the end of the afternoon. Others took pictures or wandered toward the basilica that rose at the end of the square, glowing in the afternoon light. The guidebook had warned that the San Marco cafes were ridiculously expensive, but her feet hurt from all the walking and the sight of ice cream made her hungry. She realized she had forgotten to eat lunch.

She sat at a table and ordered gelato and an espresso. They arrived, the ice cream in a large round bowl, the coffee in a tiny white cup. She slid her spoon into the gelato and tasted peaches, summer, home. The sun lit up the gold wings of the angels on top of the basilica and she sat watching, camera forgotten on the table, as children chased pigeons, couples and families lost and found each other, waiters moved among the tables like water, while elegant musicians played on violins and grand pianos and heart-strings.

She found an Internet cafe on the way home and wrote to her children:

The water is green here and smells like a quiet sea and fishes. There are no cars. The people go about in boats and the houses wear gold. I ate ice cream made from peaches in a living room as big as a lake. Someday you will see all this. I love you, Mom

By the end of the week, Sara had decided that her feet and eyes and nose were much more interesting guides than a map. Over the years, she had forgotten what it felt like to walk with the delicious purposelessness of going nowhere. But now she remembered, and she spent hours simply moving, reveling in the feeling of the muscles of her legs, the swing of her arms against her body. She stopped only to eat, or take pictures — the smooth brown leather surface of a cat mask, the light caught in its curves; the middle-aged couple oblivious to the world, sitting on a park bench, her legs draped across his lap, his fingers on her ankles. A family eating Sunday lunch, the aroma of their meal drenching the air in a scent so warm and round and golden it made breathing feel like eating.

How long had it been, she wondered, since she had seen the world like this?

One afternoon, she heard string instruments and followed the sound down a narrow passageway, through a tunnel between two buildings and into a small piazza. In the middle of the otherwise deserted square, Sara saw a man in a tuxedo and a woman in a white tulle ball dress and long white gloves. Tall, both of them, impossibly tall. On stilts, Sara realized after a moment. The couple, unaware of her presence, was pacing in long-legged strides in time with the music. Then suddenly they stopped, turned and moved forward into each other's arms. Dancing. Ballroom dancing, the woman's dress flowing out behind her, the long, thin blackness of her stilts sweeping up into the air as the man lifted her over his shoulder, a great arc of white, then landed her gently, serenely, back on the cobblestones from which she had started.

Sara watched until they stopped dancing and got down from their stilts and stood, laughing, in the middle of the piazza. She walked up to them.

"Why?" she asked simply.

"Perche no?" they replied. Why not?

Up above them, a child leaned out an upper window and clapped, her face alight with joy.

On her way back to the hotel Sara spotted an Internet cafe and went inside. Settling into a chair, surrounded by the warmth of the room and the gentle clacking of the keyboards around her, she addressed an email to her father.

She paused for a moment and then smiled. *I have an idea,* she wrote.

Then she clicked "send" and walked out into the rest of her trip.

HADLEY

Hadley's house was small, bought almost four years before with the money from her husband's life insurance policy, the one that listed "automobile accident" but never told you about the red of a car slamming out of its lane, the way life couldn't be insured, only paid for. The way the future could become a bank of clouds you couldn't fly over.

The real estate agent had shown her the house, nonchalant in her certainty that Hadley would say no. The house had, to be sure, seen better days, and even from the outside the shape suggested that the original architect had perhaps not been one at all. But for Hadley the house had been perfect, its main entrance a side one, hidden by an arbor drenched in climbing roses. Loneliness would look for a front door, Hadley thought, might not track her down the narrow bark-covered path, might get lost among the unruly green, the whispered distractions of sweet white scents. She'd paint the door, her door, a quiet blue, she decided, even before she opened it and saw inside the house.

It was a house too small for ceremony, marriage or otherwise. A side porch just big enough for taking off gardening boots, and then instantly the kitchen with its old milk-paint cupboards rising to the ceiling and an ancient apron sink with rust marking the well-worn path of water dripping from faucet to drain. An afterthought of a table with one chair nestled into a corner next to a 1930s range. A checkerboard floor of faded red-and-white linoleum, the edges of the tiles catching gently on the soles of Hadley's shoes. Beyond that, a child-sized living room looking out to a tangled mass of garden, a footnote of a bathroom, and a bedroom with a twin bed pushed against the wall to make space for a tiny dresser.

"It doesn't even fit a real bed," the real estate agent had said, shaking her head in disbelief.

Sean had been tall; a queen bed was the smallest size they could ever consider. Hadley had spent her three hundred and sixty-three married nights entangled in his limbs as his long legs reached across the mattress, searching for space like vines stretching for the sun. After the funeral Hadley had begun sleeping with pillows packed around her; it kept her from moving, waking into the recognition of his absence.

"A twin bed is fine," Hadley answered, ignoring the curiosity on her agent's face. Her agent was young — not even thirty, her bed still a playground, Hadley thought. No need to tell her it could be otherwise. No need to realize that they were likely the same age.

But as Hadley looked around the house, she found she was drawn to its diminutive proportions, the way each piece of furniture fit into a nook like the living quarters of a sailboat. A safe place, out of the weather. You could even pretend you were sailing forward.

"Are you seriously interested?" the agent asked.

"Let's see the garden," Hadley responded, as she headed back through the kitchen. But she already knew.

Hadley's friends at work had thought it strange that she bought a house. It seemed so conservative and grown-up, inconsistent with the fun-loving Hadley they had known who worked in marketing and went kayaking and biking with her boyfriend, then husband, on the weekends. It seemed odd for a woman to settle down and buy a house after her husband died. In their universe, the order was usually reversed, and preferably with a long lag time between one and the other.

But for Hadley it had all been perfectly clear. When Sean died she understood for the first time how completely human beings were dependent upon a suspension of disbelief in order simply to move forward through their days. If that suspension faltered, if you truly understood, even if only for a moment, that human beings were made of bones and blood that broke and sprayed with the slightest provocation, and that provocation was everywhere — in street curbs and dangling tree limbs, bicycles and pencils — well, you would fly for the first nest in a tree, run flat-out for the first burrow you saw.

But her friends still saw everything the old way; they crossed streets against the lights, ate hot dogs from the corner vendor who everybody knew didn't throw out his unsold product at the end of the day. It was more than Hadley could bear, to watch them. More than she could bear to sit at her desk and remember the woman who used to sit there, the woman who had a husband and who kayaked and biked on the weekends. When her boss called her into his office to offer her a leave of absence, she agreed, except she made it a permanent one. She had money saved up, for the trip she and Sean had been planning to South America. And there was more left from the insurance; the house was small, not expensive. She didn't need much. She wasn't planning on doing anything. One more move and she could be done.

Sean's mother had come to the apartment, sobbing, to take whatever of his childhood Hadley hadn't hidden in the back of dresser drawers, in the cabinet above the refrigerator.

"I know you loved him, honey," her mother-in-law said, her voice made greedy by loss, "but surely you can't want these things from when he was little. When he was my boy."

And Hadley, looking at her mother-in-law's raw and jagged grief, couldn't say yes, she did. Couldn't tell her about the nights when she had worn Sean's high school track and field letter jacket and nothing else, Sean laughing at how very much of her it covered, making hopelessly awful jokes about hurdles and endurance and pole vaulting as he undid the snaps, one by one. Couldn't say she wanted Sean's silver baby cup for the child that would not be conceived.

In the end, however, there had been relatively few things that Hadley brought with her to the new house. After her mother-in-law had left and the apartment returned to silence it seemed as if each object Hadley picked up was suddenly freighted with the heaviness of hidden fists, ready to sucker punch. A toothbrush, its bristles splayed with use. A magazine with the corner of a page turned down. The bowls, red when all the rest of their plates were white, because Sean said cereal deserved a happy color. After she had answered the phone that evening when everything changed, she'd tried to eliminate the reminders. She took the black T-shirt and jeans she had been wearing and convinced the funeral home director to sneak them in with Sean's body just before the cremation. She stayed far away from the smells of roasting chicken and lemons, smashed the dinner plates that had been set out on the table, dropping them extravagantly from the third-floor apartment window until the landlord agreed that it might be best if she were allowed to break her lease as well.

But it had turned out that reminders were like dandelions; yanking one out only seemed to grow dozens, and Hadley had found herself putting one item after another out on the curb in front of her apartment building. They were always gone by morning.

She had moved into her new house, bought plates and a twin bed at a garage sale, borrowing other people's lives, and sat on the couch in the living room for months, drinking tea and watching the garden encroach, welcoming the feeling that she was surrounded, getting smaller, buried like an acorn under the leaves.

A friend from college passed through town.

"Dear Lord, darling," she said, looking out the living room window at the garden. "They're going to need the Jaws of Life to get you out of here." A Freudian slip. It was astonishing how often they showed up, Hadley thought, as if Sean's death was an uneven step people couldn't help tripping on.

But Hadley didn't mind the unruly nature of her garden. She was safe; there wasn't a car in the world that could blast through that wall of green. She could feel the garden reaching out its arms to protect her.

Hadley had been making toast one Saturday morning in early summer when she heard a van grumbling up the driveway next door. The house had been built on speculation, the freshly laid sod around it as plain as her own garden was overgrown.

Hadley stepped out the kitchen door and heard the sound of a young boy's voice, muffled at first by the closed windows of a car, then let loose into the world.

"Mom, look! It's a secret garden!"

And within a moment, she heard the sounds of something large and heavy being dragged across the yard and landing hard against her fence.

"Tyler!" a woman's voice called out. "What are you doing?"

"Looking!"

Hadley heard the boy's voice muttering as the object shifted against the fence, and then a head popped over the top of the boards. The face looked to be about six years old, towheaded, both hair and skin showing the remains of a peanut butter sandwich. The boy stared at Hadley, who stared back.

"I live here now," the boy said, finally.

"So do I," replied Hadley.

The boy looked about. "I think there are fairies in your garden."

"Maybe." Hadley had to admit there had been times she'd had the same thought, usually late at night, when a scent she couldn't identify floated in the open kitchen door.

"I'm sorry." A woman's head joined the boy's, a newborn cradled against her shoulder. "Is he bothering you?" she said, nodding toward her son.

"Not at all," replied Hadley, feeling the wheel of politeness creak slowly into motion.

The woman's smile was relieved.

"I'm Sara," she said. "The ringmaster of this traveling circus. This is my son Tyler, and that's my husband, Dan." She nodded across the yard toward the house, where a young man, another baby in his arms, was trying to open the front door of the house for the movers.

"We thought we'd be in the house before the twins came," Sara said, a bit apologetically, but whether the apology was to Hadley or the babies, Hadley couldn't tell.

One morning, about a week after Sara and Dan moved in, Hadley had been trying to muscle open a reluctant living room window

178

when she heard the babies crying next door, first one, and then both. Hadley went outside and looked over the fence. Across her neighbor's yard, she saw Sara through the curtainless living room window, walking in her bathrobe, holding a nursing baby in one arm, while attempting to balance the other on her shoulder. Hadley started to draw back from the intimacy of the scene but she saw Tyler at the window, looking out toward Hadley's house. He spotted her and waved.

Hadley found herself walking across the grass in Sara's yard, the damp blades cool against the soles of her bare feet. Tyler came and opened the back door.

"The babies have been awake forever," he said simply.

Hadley entered the living room; Sara saw her and merely nodded, any personal need to apologize for the bedlam of her household long gone in the fog of her exhaustion.

Hadley crossed the room and took the extra baby — the boy, she figured, seeing the blue sleeper-suit. She brought the small body up to her shoulder, patting his back. He smelled soft and warm, like flour that had been left in the sun. She could feel the waves of his sobs as the sound blasted near her ear. Instinctively, she took him outside,

179

where the fresh air startled him momentarily into stillness.

"That's a good boy," Hadley said, rubbing his back. "See how nice it is."

Tyler followed her and stood, his hand touching her elbow.

"That's Max," he commented. "The other one's Hillary. They cry a lot."

"Well," Hadley responded, thinking about it. "It must be hard not to be able to talk. Do you remember what that was like?"

Tyler shook his head.

"Me neither," said Hadley. "But I bet it's lousy."

She moved her feet gently, back and forth in rhythm with the breeze outside. The baby burrowed into the warmth of her body, settling against her chest, his head resting on her shoulder. Every once in a while the shudder of an almost-forgotten sob ruffled his body and she would press her hand against his back, letting his movement sink into her body.

"I'm going to check on Mom. I'll tell her you're okay," Tyler said, his voice grown-up and companionable.

Hadley walked the baby over to her yard. The roses cascaded off the wooden arbor in huge curtains of white. She opened the gate and walked inside the garden, over to an old blue garden chair that was just barely holding its own against the overgrowth of ivy. Holding the baby firmly with one arm, she bent over and swept off a layer of dried leaves and sat down, sinking into the deep embrace of the chair. The garden was quiet; soft, forgotten scents filtered down from the arbor and up through the overgrowth around her. The baby relaxed, his body lowering into sleep. She could feel the heat of his body against her chest as he sank deeper, the way the warmth seemed to open her ribs, leave room for her lungs.

An hour or so later Hadley woke to the sound of the gate opening. Sara stood there, smiling.

"Tyler *said* there were fairies in your garden," she commented.

After Sara left with Max, Hadley had walked back into her kitchen, running her fingertips along the countertops and the rounded handle of the old refrigerator, feeling for changes. Because things *had* changed, the air warmer, quieter somehow. She felt stronger than she had in a long time.

She paused in the middle of the kitchen, turning to tell Sean, and then realized what she was doing.

■ ■ ■ ■

After that, it had been the most natural thing in the world to cross the yard, pick up a baby, stir a pot on the stove. Whatever needed doing.

"You are a lifesaver," Sara said. "What can I do for you?"

"This," Hadley answered, and she had bought a small blue wooden step, just high enough that Tyler could reach the latch on her gate.

About three weeks after Sara had moved in, a woman had arrived at Hadley's door, introducing herself as Marion and asking if Hadley wanted to join a baby-holding circle for Sara. Although Hadley had not been excited about the concept of joining anything, a feeling of protectiveness rose up in her — she was hardly going to let Max and Hillary go into hands she didn't know — and so she agreed. Marion also roped in her younger sister, Daria, a choice that Hadley questioned the first time she met her, but Daria melted into the twins and quickly became a favorite. Marion's friend Caroline suggested her friend Kate. And there they were — five women, one for each weekday.

Eventually, Hadley had come to know all of them. It was Marion who started the tradition of stopping by Hadley's after her shift, for a cup of tea if it was morning, or a glass of wine if she had a late afternoon slot. One by one, the other women followed suit until sometimes Hadley wondered, not always gratefully, just whom the circle was holding. But over the months she came to look forward to these visits, the way the edges of the women were softened by their time with the babies, their voices becoming lower and more melodious, words caressing things they loved rather than darting out at the world's frustrations.

Of course, they all wanted to set her up with someone.

"Hadley, you're young. You're gorgeous," Daria had remarked early one evening. "You should be going out and seeing people. Men." Daria liked the afternoon shifts with the twins; they allowed her a full day working at her pottery studio and then a chance to unwind with the babies, as she put it, before going out in the evening. Daria said there was no aphrodisiac for men like the look in a woman's eyes after she had been holding a baby.

"It's like we're just radiating pheromones or something," Daria said. "You should use this to your advantage. Find a guy — at least have sex."

"I'm fine," Hadley replied. "I don't need anyone right now." Hadley had wondered why it was so important to all of them. Truly, she was so much better than she had been after Sean died. She simply didn't have an interest in men anymore. It wasn't that she didn't like them; she just knew how easily they broke.

"But don't you want this?" Caroline asked one morning, nodding her chin down toward the sleeping baby in her arms. She had come over, bringing little Hillary with her.

"No," Hadley lied.

One afternoon, almost a year after the women had started the baby-holding circle, Kate and Hadley had been sitting in Hadley's kitchen. Hadley was making tea, watching the steam rise, the way the hot water lured clouds of brown tea from the bags. As Hadley poured milk into a small pitcher Kate turned to her.

"I have something to tell you," she said.

Hadley nodded, concentrating on the milk, the way the white of the liquid met the white of the pitcher, the two so similar and yet if you paid attention you could see

184

the difference. She knew what Kate was going to say; she had seen the change in Kate's face over the months, the way her eyes had darkened, pulling in her thoughts. You could tell, the same way you could tell if a woman was pregnant. The opposite of glow.

"They think they've caught it early," Kate said. "They say I should be just fine."

Hadley waited, listening. She remembered the way people used to talk and talk when she told them what had happened to Sean, as if words would somehow fill up the space that suddenly gaped around her. What she had wanted was silence. But now, listening to Kate, it was as if she could hear the brakes screaming, the sound of the impact as fate hit her friend and sent her life flying. No wonder people wanted to talk.

"I knew this would be hard for you; I wanted to tell you myself," said Kate. She looked outside to the garden, away from Hadley. The kitchen was quiet. "It's so green," Kate said, almost to herself.

"We're changing the baby-holding circle," Marion had told Hadley. "The twins are a year old; Sara's got it under control. It's time to take care of Kate."

Hadley felt her chin pull back, an involuntary movement.

"It's too soon," she said. Her voice sounded childlike, even to her, but she didn't know what else to say.

She had been waiting, the way the books and her mother on the phone and the nurse at the hospital that night had said. They said it would get better, day by day. And it had. Each day was one more stick in the bridge she was making over the crevasse of Sean's death. One more thing to stand on. But all it took, apparently, was one piece of news, one small sideswipe of someone else's life and you were standing on the edge again, your stomach already falling.

"I'm not ready," she said.

Marion nodded. "When do you think you would be?" she asked, her voice calm and nonjudgmental.

Hadley stopped; she couldn't imagine.

"You know," Marion said, "I met a woman once when I was a teenager. I knew she had gone through a lot, but she was so strong, so compassionate. I asked her how she could be the way she was, and you know what she told me?"

Hadley shook her head.

"She said, 'You can be broken, or broken open. That choice is yours.' "

After her talk with Marion, Hadley had

gone to the hardware store and bought a long-handled lopper. When she got home, she chopped a space out of the ivy that surrounded the chair, a rough frame to the chaos around it. Still, it was space. When Kate saw it, she laughed.

"Any port in a storm, Hadley," she said.

After that, Kate often came to Hadley's house after her treatments. Kate would fall asleep in the big blue chair in the garden and Hadley would sit and watch the ivy grow around her. And every time after Kate went home, Hadley would cut it back again.

For eighteen months the women had held tight around Kate, as if simply by their existence they could form a boundary that would hold her inside when it seemed everything else was trying to pull her away. But Kate hadn't died, had stayed inside the circle, and after the last test results had come back stunningly, miraculously clean, they all had met that September evening for Kate's victory party. And when Kate had told Hadley that her challenge was to take care of her garden, there wasn't a single woman at the table who was surprised.

It was a morning in late March. Hadley stood at her back door, looking out at the green sea that was her backyard. The ivy flowed over shapes that might have once been bushes, swirled up the trunk of the plum tree and along its branches, crept up the walls of the house and edged across the windows. It was easy to be seduced by the lushness of it all, to be overwhelmed by the determination that carried it green and thriving through winter when so many plants cut loose their leaves and sent their roots hustling deeper into the ground at the first sign of cold weather. Hadley had promised Kate that she would take care of her garden, but she had delayed, daunted by the task, watching as the ivy came closer, winding its way along the path and up the porch. As she stood on her back porch, Hadley glanced down to see a tendril casually reaching out for the doorknob.

She walked resolutely into the kitchen and found the gardening gloves Marion had given her. Then she went outside, hearing the screen door close reluctantly behind her.

"Okay," she said, and put on her gloves.

She started at the back door, unraveling the serpentine vines that traveled up the porch railings toward the house. The soft green tips came loose easily under her fingers, but it was only a matter of a foot or two before the tendrils hardened, their glossy leaves hiding clusters of threads tenaciously latched onto the wood. Pulling them off left footprints of suckers and brought away chunks of paint.

Well, Hadley thought, I needed to repaint anyway.

And she pulled, dropping the leggy strands into a pile that grew until her only option was to get rid of it. She dragged an old black plastic trashcan from the garage and plunged her hands into the mountain of discarded ivy, shoving in armload after armload. When the can was full, she climbed in, using the railing for support, and stomped down with her feet until there was room for more. When she could cram no further, she gripped the can with both hands and dragged it to the curb out front and returned.

An hour later, Hadley stepped back and looked at the porch. Ripped clean of its vegetative covering, it had a slightly scarred quality, its white paint mottled with bare patches and ivy threads, the area around it bare. But its lines rose clean and straight from the ground, claiming its space. A firm place to stand on, she thought as she looked at it — part inside, part out. She wondered who the architect was who had first understood that basic human need to have a place, a moment, to pause before entering, to shift from the person you were outside to the one you would become when you walked through the door.

She hadn't gotten that, she thought, looking at the porch — when Sean died, there had just been before the phone call and after. No illness, no aging. Just Sean and then no Sean. No porch to stand on, to get ready to go inside.

I needed a porch, she thought.

She stood hot and dirty in the early spring air, looking out at the garden. Above the tidal wave of green she could just make out the tops of the plum tree branches.

"My yard," she said, looking at the ivy. "Not yours."

She took off her sweatshirt, then picked the first vine she could distinguish from the tangle on the ground and yanked; it gave way with a quick snap and a spray of dirt and dust, leaving her holding a piece some five feet long. She'd never win like that, she thought. She chose a new strand and pulled, slowly and steadily this time, drawing it toward her hand over hand, feeling the tension grow as she worked her way down the vine. She closed her eyes and increased the pressure as she felt resistance, feeling only the hard line of energy between them, the rope of the vine through the gloves on her hands. She pulled, hard. Somewhere, deep in the undergrowth, the ivy was giving up, unlatching from the ground at its very source. She was almost there.

There was a crack and she flew backward, landing hard on her tailbone. She swore loudly, not caring who heard her. It felt good. She opened her eyes, stood up and grabbed another vine and then another and another. The muscles in her arms and legs grew warm as she worked; her mouth became gritty from the dust and dirt that flew through the air. She worked, not thinking, time measured in huge paper yard bags — one, two, three, four.

After hauling the fourth bag to the front curb, she took a break. She was hungry, her body demanding food. She made a sandwich and brought her plate outside, sitting on the porch steps in the cool air, taking huge, gratifying bites of turkey and bread, sweating slightly and looking out proudly over her progress. She could do this, she thought. It wasn't such a big deal.

The sun had changed position as she worked and was shining down through the leaves in the back of her yard. She had always wondered what kind of trees lined the fence — their trunks were hardy, the branches thick as her arm. The ivy didn't stand a chance against them, and the thought had always brought her hope. She had looked forward to clearing the space around the trees, giving them more room to grow. Now, between the sun and her efforts, she could truly make them out for the first time. Her gaze idly followed the patterns of vines climbing up them.

No, not up them, she realized with a start — from them. The trees *were* ivy.

"Oh no." The words came out of Hadley's mouth, small and quiet. She stood up, her hands shaking, took the sandwich to the kitchen and placed it carefully on the counter. Then she walked to the bathroom, stripped off her clothes and got into her tiny shower. She sat on the floor, her back against the cold tile wall, her face in her hands, feeling the water falling over her head.

Hadley woke up the next morning to the sound of voices in her yard. Her head ached and her eyes still felt swollen. What time was it? She reached over to check the clock, feeling the creak and growl of her muscles, the blood still heavy in her head. Nine A.M. Who was in her yard? Maybe the ivy had really taken over, grown legs and voices and was coming for her house. It didn't seem impossible.

The voices became louder, laughing.

She pulled on her bathrobe, wincing when she reached her left arm back to find the sleeve, and then walked gingerly to the kitchen door.

They were all there — Sara and Dan and Tyler and the twins, Kate and Caroline, Marion and her husband, Terry, Daria and Henry. Marion held up a machete, Dan a chain saw.

"We're bringing in the big guns," Tyler said stoutly.

It was as if she had been gardening with fingernail scissors the day before. As she watched, the sharp blade of the machete flung aside curtains of ivy while the chain saw ripped through branches. The ivy, so invulnerable the day before, seemed to melt in the face of so much concerted energy. In front of her eyes, the climate of her backyard was changing from shade to sunshine.

They worked in pairs, cutting and bagging. They took turns filling water bottles and passing them around, or taking care of the twins, who, unlike Tyler, were not enthralled with the scream of motorized tools. At one point Caroline convinced Dan to let her use the chain saw, wielding it with great satisfaction against the trunk of one of the ivy trees.

When she was done she passed the chain saw into Hadley's hands. "Try it," she shouted over the noise of the machine. "It feels great."

The machine vibrated and bucked slightly, just barely in control; it was like holding on to the handlebars of a mountain bike while flying down a steep and rutted trail. Dan slapped a pair of goggles over Hadley's eyes and pointed to another ivy tree, giving her a thumbs-up.

She put the edge of the blade against the trunk of the tree and felt it buck back.

"You gotta commit," Caroline yelled, laughing.

Hadley tried again and felt the blade dig into the hard surface, chewing its way through. As she reached the far side of the trunk, a canopy of branches and limbs fell to the side and sunlight rushed into the opening.

Dan took the saw back and turned it off. The garden vibrated in the sudden silence.

"Come on," Caroline said to Hadley, "let's pull this sucker out of here." And they grabbed two of the larger branches and

194

dragged their prize out to the truck Terry had waiting at the curb.

Six hours later, they all stopped and gazed about them.

"It looks great," Marion declared.

"It looks like a clear-cut," Daria snorted.

"Let's call it a clean slate," Caroline corrected with a smile. Looking at her, Hadley thought how much Caroline had changed in the past months, her hair short now, her eyes clear and honest.

That said, Hadley had to admit that Daria had a point about the clear-cut. It was hard even to guess the names of the pitiful combination of bushes and bedraggled plants that had emerged from under the ivy.

"There's a whole world still in there," Marion said. "You'll be amazed what you find when you get into the details. See the roses in the back?" She pointed toward the fence. Sure enough, Hadley could see the leggy stems of a rose, climbing up the post.

"Dinnertime!" Sara came to the open gate, Max on her hip.

"It smells fantastic," Caroline said. The scent of butter and truffles drifted across the yard from Sara's house.

"You should see our dinners since Sara got back from Italy," Dan commented happily.

"Here's to a day well spent," Kate toasted, lifting her glass of red wine.

Platters of pasta and bowls of salad were passed around the table along with the twins, who traveled from one lap to the next, mouths ready to catch the bites that were sent in their direction. Tyler had chosen a permanent seat next to Hadley, who sat, still slightly in shock from the accomplishment and affection of the day.

"Mom's been reading me *The Secret Garden*," Tyler said to her.

"Really? I loved that story when I was a kid." Hadley had a sudden image of the backyard of her childhood, its hidden alcoves and the woods that rambled away from its edge.

"Usually secret gardens are for kids," Tyler noted sagely.

"Secret gardens are for whoever finds them," Sara commented from the other side of the table. "But I'm sure Hadley will share."

Marion came over a few days after the clear-cut. Hadley watched as Marion's eyes gazed about the yard, detecting patterns.

"How old was the woman who lived

here?" Marion asked.

"Eighty or so, I think. The agent told me she'd been here forty years."

Marion smiled. "You can tell. It's an old garden. There's a lot more roses than I thought."

Hadley looked closely and saw the browned, curled edges of a rose blossom.

"And there's her kitchen garden." Marion pointed to the corner closest to the house where Hadley could just make out a rectangle, about five feet by ten feet, bordered by smooth, round rocks the size of her fist. And that was a tomato cage, she realized, lolled up against the side of the house.

"The plants would get the southern sun there," Marion continued. "Now, I would bet . . ." She made her way toward the kitchen garden along a brick path, almost invisible under a coating of black mold, then stopped abruptly. "Yes! I figured she'd put herbs along the walkway. See?"

Hadley bent down. It was all a mass of seemingly dead sticks and stems, a leaf here or there, no two the same. But as Marion's fingers moved from one to the next, pointing out distinctions, Hadley saw the tiny pointed leaves of thyme and a broad silvery oval of sage. Hadley touched first one, then another, laughing softly as the scents were released into the air.

Hadley sank her spade into the soil, loosening the roots of the weeds that had taken hold around the base of the plum tree. She wondered sometimes what she was doing, digging up the insistent survivors, the dandelions whose roots sank down like surveyors' stakes into the ground, the frothy green lace that suddenly appeared, floating tenaciously over the surface of everything, turning red as it established its reign. But there were green shoots sprouting as well — tulips and hyacinths and irises. She wanted to give them room.

The garden was taking shape. A few days after the clear-cut, Hadley and Tyler had cleaned the mold from the brick pathway. Tyler had pretended he was a pirate prisoner, forced to scrub the decks. Hadley claimed the role of Cinderella, left behind by her cruel stepsisters to wash the kitchen floors. As their brushes worked down into the cracks of the bricks, a warm red color appeared, lightening to a friendly orange as it dried.

"Now," Tyler had said, standing back proudly to survey their work, "you have a safe path to take you between the alligator-infested waters."

And Hadley had started from the safe path, working back foot by foot into the garden. Over the weeks, the chaos had receded, giving way to soft dirt, small mysteries like welcome notes sent from the old woman who had once tended the garden. Day lilies and wild geraniums and tufted primroses, sage with its silvery leaves, the green spikes of rosemary and the blue-gray leaves of lavender, slowly, one by one, rising up out of the earth as Hadley cleared the way around them. She found she could spend hours filtering the clumps of dirt into smooth soil, cutting back the dead stalks of roses that grew gratefully, greedily after she had tended them. Life between her fingers.

She had come to love the soft spring rain, when the ground opened up to the water from the sky, and the roots of the weeds came out easily in her fingers. She bought a big rain hat and coat; Marion said it made her look like a yellow mushroom, but she didn't care. She delighted in the feeling of being in her own dry shelter as the moisture slid across the slope of her hat and down the back of her rain slicker. She welcomed the sight of her green rain boots waiting for her on the back porch when she returned from the grocery store, like dogs anxious for a walk. Some days, when the rain came down soft around her, she felt as thirsty for it as the earth beneath her feet.

One day she found an old nest, tucked in a crook of the plum tree. She went and found the rock that Kate had given her and placed it in the nest, where it lay like a smooth black egg.

"Have you noticed something odd about this garden?" Hadley commented to Marion one afternoon. Marion had come over, tools in hand, for a little "gardening therapy," as she called it. Why Marion needed another garden Hadley could never quite determine, as Marion had a large and well-established one of her own, but Hadley chose not to point that out. As much as anything, Hadley realized, she wanted to stay near the maternal assurance that Marion radiated. Hadley's own mother had come for the week after Sean's death, but she had a job and the rest of the family on the East Coast. She had tried to convince Hadley to move home, but Hadley couldn't bring herself to leave. Being with Marion helped her feel a bit more like here was home.

"What do you mean by odd?" Marion asked.

"Well, it seems like almost all the flowers that were planted in this garden are white."

"Hmmm . . ." Marion smiled. "I think we may have a night garden on our hands."

"A night garden?"

"It's meant to be seen at night. Moonlight, in particular. Interesting choice in a rainy climate."

"Do you ever wonder about her? The woman who planted this?"

"It's hard not to." Marion shook the extra dirt from her gloves. "She's everywhere you look. You can tell so much about a person by the garden they plant."

"What do you mean?"

"Well, I know she was thrifty and probably a good cook because of how much space she gave to her kitchen garden. On the other hand, what kind of woman grows a night garden? Did she work during the day? Was she an insomniac? Or maybe she was just a complete romantic."

"I never thought of it that way."

"Once you start looking, it's hard to stop. You can tell more about a person from their garden than you ever will from what they say about themselves."

It was true, Hadley realized. She had taken Tyler and the twins for walks around the neighborhood for years now, but after her talk with Marion, Hadley began observing her neighbors' gardens as she walked, a fascinating activity, as intimate as reading their mail. There was the woman on the corner, the quiet member of a large and noisy family, her house hidden by bowers of honeysuckle, surrounded by pale lavender and sage, pastel flowers asking only for sympathy. Next door was The Fence, imposing and blank; one day when the gate was mistakenly left open, however, Hadley had seen inside a garden of such abundance that she stopped, shocked. Some yards were planted as if with plans for long tenancy, others created with the impulse buys and on-sale annuals found near the checkout stands. Some people had their gardens taken care of for them, never feeling dirt between their fingers. The more time Hadley spent in her garden, the more she wondered what she would do without that feeling and the way it held her to the ground, gave her something to stand on.

Now, Hadley found herself taking walks simply to see the next garden, the next story, lives opening up before her. Tyler didn't always come with her. He was busier now; his grandfather was staying with them for the summer and these days when Hadley worked in her garden she could hear the sounds of construction coming from the garage next door, the excited exchange of voices between grandfather and grandson. But Tyler still came with her on her walks sometimes, his insights filtering through his eight-year-old eyes.

"That one, for sure, was a pirate before he bought a house," Tyler said, gesturing toward a tall, thin house set far back in a narrow lot, its top floor peering out above the tops of the trees. "And I bet that lady" — he pointed to a well-manicured lawn, its edges precise, the flower beds planted in rows of annuals — "makes cookies every night, but they don't taste very good."

Hadley found it hard to describe what she had been seeing in her walks, feeling in her garden. The way the roses in her arbor bent down to caress the top of her head as she walked underneath them to her door. The first frilly tops of the carrots in her kitchen garden coming up to greet her, each moment of green making her stand a little straighter with the knowledge that she could make her own food. The glow of the white palette that surrounded her house, pulling her outside as the sky began to fade, tempting her to sit or work in the yard and listen to the neighborhood around her, the families coming together, settling down. Sometimes her garden felt like a benevolent parent who seemed to know what she needed before she did.

She tried to explain to Marion as they sat on the porch steps one afternoon, fresh mint from the shady part of the garden flavoring their glasses of iced tea.

"I wonder what it would be like to design a garden to take care of a person," Hadley commented.

Marion smiled. "Have you ever thought about becoming a landscape designer?"

Hadley shook her head, but the thought didn't dislodge with the action. It stayed with her, insistent as a small child, leading her by the hand to the local community college where she signed up for summer classes.

Hadley found to her surprise that as much as she liked the actual tending of plants, she liked learning about the creation of gardens even more. She was quickly absorbed in the intricate equation of soil and water and light, the constantly shifting dance of fragrance and color palettes. As she learned to see gardens as stories that unfurled over spring, summer, fall and winter, landscapes became fluid, the plants within them developing their own personalities over the course of a year or a decade. There were the annuals, blasting their way through the spring and summer with a blaze of color and produce, ramming straight into the wall of winter without any thought other than reproduction; the perennials, pulling back into the ground as cold approached, then reappearing again in an elaborate game of horticultural hide-and-seek; the weeds, their desire for life so strong that daily growth had to be measured in feet, not inches. Creating an aesthetic harmony in the midst of such abundance was far more complicated than she had ever imagined, yet she dove into the particulars with the first real happiness she had felt since Sean died, tumbling into the beauty of a tall blue iris set against a pink rose, the soft, feathery grace of pale yellow columbine draping over the edge of a shaded stone walkway.

At the end of the day, she would come home to her own garden and walk into its lush green, the cool white of its flowers. If the day had been warm, she would turn on a sprinkler and sit outside as the evening air softened around her and the plants stretched up, green and alive. Afterward, she would move along the narrow walkways of her garden, artemisia and sweet woodruff brushing wet against her ankles as she leaned over to cut a huge teacup of a rose for her kitchen table.

One evening she noticed that a vine growing along the back fence had developed
what looked like long green tubes. The vine
had shown up one day, seemingly out of
nowhere, but it had quickly and conve-
niently covered the rough edges of the
chopped ivy and she had let it be. Now she
looked at it, wondering what would come
next. As she watched, the moon came out
and one of the pale green tubes rose as if to
music, unwinding slowly like a pinwheel,
spreading, extending, opening into a great
white flower the size of her outstretched
hand.

And then the heat wave came, unexpected
and out of character for the Pacific Northwest. Without air-conditioning, people made
do with portable fans, propping them on
kitchen counters and in windows, anything
to push the molten air.

Gardens gasped. The days were too long,
the length of time between water seemingly
infinite. The regal stems of her daisy plants
were dragged to the ground by the weight
of their flowers. The leaves on the plum tree
curled up in fetal positions.

People retreated into more primal behav-
iors as well — etiquette and good humor

pitched aside like candy wrappers. Clothes became just another trap to hold the heat, and in the mornings Hadley found herself moving past the jeans and T-shirts in her closet to pull out sundresses she hadn't worn in years. She would walk up the stairs to the school, the gauzy fabric whispering across the surface of her skin and fanning the air around her bare legs. After school she would buy a soda from the vending machine and drive home, holding the cold can between her breasts. She would return to a house that had soaked up the calidity of the day and then held it jealously long into the night. Even with every window open, the rooms seemed to vibrate. Hadley lay in her twin bed, her arms and legs outstretched beyond its boundaries. The heat hung about her and she was filled with a desire to take down the wall between the living room and bedroom, to make one open space where the air could move and she could see the garden from her bed.

On the third night, Hadley finally gave up on sleep and went outside. It was almost midnight and the city around her had grown quiet, a miraculous occurrence in a city that always had the growl of a freeway in the distance or the sound of children playing in the yards. Out on the street, a car went by, windows down, jazz music playing, and then nothing. The streetlamp out front flickered off, leaving only the moon.

It took a moment for Hadley's eyes to adjust, the white of the tiny sweet woodruff flowers and the huge and luxurious petals of the roses coming first, and then the silver of the sage and lamb's ears, and finally the deeper greens, the outline of leaves and lacy edges aided by the faint glow from the kitchen. The garden lay before her, waiting.

She had watered earlier that evening, the sprinkler head still at the end of the long black hose that ran in sinuous curves across the thyme and along the path between the lilies to the plum tree. The plants didn't really need any more water, but she could feel the desire for it in her skin and the heaviness of her limbs. She turned on the faucet and then breathed in the smell of thyme that was released by the water, a scent of evergreen and citrus and innocence, a cool green place in the midst of the heat. Hadley stepped into the arcs of flying drops, feeling them land and slide across her skin. She stretched her arms up into the branches of the plum tree and let the water fall down the long, straight column that was her body.

MARION

When Marion had been a teenager, she wanted a tattoo. As an oldest child who did mostly what was expected of her, she had been fascinated by the abandon tattoos implied, the willing, blind leap into commitment. Whether or not she was the type to make such a bold declaration was, in the end, inconsequential. Her parents had forbidden her to get one, a decision that would not have changed even with the most passionate or logical of defenses, which she didn't mount in any case. Perhaps that was a sign. Perhaps, as her mother said, she simply didn't understand the concept of permanence.

Her sister Daria, of course, had done it differently when she reached adolescence, had gotten tattoos even before she left home for good. She had told Marion about walking defiantly in the door, designs uncovered, the skin still red and inflamed. Daria's tattoos were always a little unsettling — a butterfly, sweet until you saw the torn wing. A snake's head sneaking out from the edge of her T-shirt sleeve. She collected tattoos like personal journal entries, a constantly updating record of her life. When Marion asked her what it was like to have strangers read your diary, Daria declared she didn't care who saw them. That was Daria, Marion thought, putting secrets on the outside to distract you from the ones within.

But Marion had never wanted a gallery of ink. She had always wanted the one image, the one that was, in fact, her essence, but that image had never settled, never stayed, which made her parents' refusal to let her get a tattoo a relief as much as anything — and before she had even noticed, life sped up and the idea of a tattoo had been lost in the chaos of college and Terry and marriage.

After the children arrived, it seemed as if life became its own skin artist — the scar on Marion's knee where she had caught it on a carpet tack while chasing after her crawling baby daughter, their laughter flying after them like flags. The cut on Terry's hand from the slip of a knife while showing the children how to make marshmallow roasting sticks on a camping trip that they all agreed was bloodier and more exciting than the *Die Hard* movie the kids had wanted to stay home and watch. The little white line, still hiding in the soft curve under her son's lip, from the time he had tripped while learning how to walk, doing the toddler-stagger down a sidewalk that suddenly felt far more like a hill as he spun forward, his small, perfect teeth cutting through the tender skin. The memory the sight of the scar always invoked in Marion — the way she had held him, the two of them nestled in the big living room chair until the small shivers of fright and worry relaxed and the sound of her voice reading a book became a river they could float down until he fell asleep.

She knew some people who railed against the marks that experience left on their bodies. To Marion, they were comforting — signs of dangers survived and past, a visual history of their family life together.

She didn't need a self-inflicted record, Marion had said when Daria showed her her newest creation. But she wondered sometimes, now that the children were gone, if that one tattoo still existed, if she would know if she saw it after so many years of not looking.

When Kate assigned Marion the challenge

of getting a tattoo, that night of Kate's victory party, Marion had been surprised, but mostly because Kate had guessed at something that Marion had only been playing with in her mind. Marion wondered at the time about Kate's ability to figure out what each of the women in the group seemed to need. They had all spent so much time taking care of Kate — but maybe, Marion had thought as she observed Kate handing out the challenges, the watching hadn't been all one way.

"Of course you are writing an article about tattoos," Daria said. It was an evening in late June. The two sisters were sitting on the deck of Henry's houseboat, looking out over the water.

"What do you mean?"

"You wouldn't just get a tattoo; you'd have to write about it. Besides, it's a great way to stall." Daria sent a good-natured grin flying out toward the small lights visible across the water.

Marion looked over at her appraisingly.

"Henry's been good for you," she commented.

"So what do you want to ask?" Daria held up her arm and pulled back her sleeve. Marion could just barely see the black and red and green markings on her sister's skin, the designs blurred in the dim light.

"Is why too obvious a question?"

Daria nodded. "And everybody's got a different answer, anyway."

"You aren't the only person I'll ask."

"I know." Daria's fingers played over the design on her right forearm, tracing loops and spirals.

Marion waited. As a journalist, she was used to this part, the way some people circled around an answer like a dog getting ready to sleep. She had learned to sit quietly, letting the space around her question expand. Beyond the edge of the dock, the water lapped against the boats moored nearby.

"You know," Daria said finally, "the first time the needles went into me, I remember thinking they felt just like Mom."

"So, how was Daria?" Terry asked as he and Marion lay in bed that night.

Marion just picked up one of his hands and kissed it.

"Is there anything you can do?" Terry's voice was supportive, genuine, but Marion noted with an inward smile how his hand moved down to her hip as he spoke, pulling her protectively closer to him. It was one of the things she loved about Terry, all the different messages he could send at one time, the many languages they could speak to each other. She leaned into what he wasn't saying and saw his eyes light in response.

Marion had first met Terry at a college friend's wedding, more than thirty years before. She had flown west, to a city of lakes and mountains she had never seen before. Her friend had been nervous, suddenly unsure of her decision; the idea of marriage, which had appeared so alluring on the brink of the uncertain future of college graduation, suddenly looking more like the longest textbook ever assigned in a freshman seminar. But Marion and the other bridesmaids had calmed her down with the confident näiveté of women who had never been married themselves and got her to the altar to become part of a couple who would, in fact, divorce ten years later.

But no one knew that then, and on the walk back up the aisle, out of the church, Marion had seen a man looking at her with such clear and honest intensity that it was all she could do not to step out of line and walk over to put her hand in his.

Thirty-three years, three children, four dogs, and one thousand three hundred thirty-five batches of Saturday pancakes later, they could still hear each other.

It all could have been different, Marion knew. She and Terry had watched so many couples fall apart after their children left, as if the ever-present urgency of their offsprings' needs had been ropes that held the boats of their separate lives together. How easy it would be, without the children's presence, to float out on currents you hadn't even realized existed, drifting idly away from each other. How easy to lock your eyes on the back of your departing child, or turn them toward the job you had always wanted, the graceful movement of a body you didn't know — sweeping your gaze over and past the spouse standing next to you.

"So," Terry said, sliding his hand up to the soft skin under her collarbone, "did Daria give you any good ideas for tattoos?"

It was just like Seattle to have the only heat wave in its history on the day of a tattoo convention, Marion thought, sweating already at ten in the morning. She put on a flowing skirt that would, she hoped, cover as much of the skin on her legs as possible. There was nothing she could do about the pristine surface of her arms; it was too hot for sleeves, although it would have been nice to maintain some feeling of mystery. No

215

secrets today; her bare arms screamed bystander, voyeur.

As far as advertising went, the tattoo convention was a bit mysterious itself, the location more hinted at than described in the literature, situated somewhere in one of the dozens of buildings at the Seattle Center, a sprawling mix of park and fountains, opera and ballet and theater auditoriums, mostly left over from a World's Fair decades before. Marion wandered about, looking for directional signs.

Coming toward her was a young man with an orange and black tiger, teeth bared, running down the length of his bicep, black metal gauges in his earlobes creating huge round holes. Marion wondered if a faraway object would look larger if she viewed it through one of them, like a telescope, but decided not to try. The young man gazed about him, slightly confused.

"Are you looking for the tattoo convention?" Marion asked.

He turned to her. Marion readied herself for sarcasm, the cynicism of the indoctrinated for the novice, but his face was merely curious.

"Yeah. Do you know where it is?"

"No, I was hoping you might."

"My friend would know. He's here, but I

can't get him to answer his cell. It gets pretty loud in there."

They stood, looking about them.

"I'm going to guess over there," Marion said, pointing across the swath of green grass to a collection of low buildings between the more imposing structures of the opera hall and the sports arena.

The young man nodded and fell into step next to her.

"Are you getting inked today?" he asked.

"Just research. For an article."

"You're a writer?"

"Journalist."

"Words, then." His stride was long and easy as they crossed the grass through crowds of summer tourists wearing shorts and baseball caps, children playing in the fountain. "So I suppose you want to know why I do it?"

They were nearing the convention; Marion could hear the music pounding its way out of the walls of the building.

"Yes."

"Irreversible decisions are good for the soul, word lady."

He gave her a quick salute and melted into the crowd in front of them, the ink on his skin as good as camouflage.

■ ■ ■ ■

Marion's fascination with tattoos had always come from the stories that were held within the ink — the ones that were obvious, slamming into your vision with the force of a well-aimed fist, or the secret messages that hid, slipping out only for the moment it took for a shirtsleeve to move, a skirt to flutter. There were the invitations — a vine of leaves, symbols in a language she didn't know, meandering down the lower backs of the women in her yoga class, disappearing under a smooth line of spandex; the warnings — the devils and screaming skulls, their intent as clear as the hair rising on a dog's back; the travelogues and merit badges and memorials; the products still on the shelf long past their expiration date.

It was the last — the tattooed names and images now regretted, rendered by time simply into symbols of one's own mutability — that had caused her to continue moving forward in her life without committing any part of it to ink. Those tattoos always reminded her of sophomore year in college, when she came across a short story she had written the year before. The mere act of seeing the typeface on the title page had brought back the excitement she had felt as the words first poured onto the page and the characters opened their souls in front of her. She turned to the first words of the story and started reading — only to be shocked by what she suddenly perceived as the immaturity of the thoughts on the page. Could she possibly have ever been so young? She tore up the story, relieved that no one other than her professor and a friend or two had seen it. For a year after that she had written nothing, paralyzed by the prospect of her future self, the thought that people would read her stories and see her as someone she had ceased to be, her writing something that she had grown beyond even as the ink sank into the page.

Journalism had helped break the block and had been her creative outlet and source of income for more than thirty years since. For some reason, people saw articles as facts caught in their own time, profiles as verbal photographs allowed to yellow with age. It had never bothered her that what she wrote as a journalist was dispensable; she was satisfied being a thought in someone's day if it left room for her to grow into the next one. She was a chronicler of life as it was lived in that moment.

Marion checked her purse for her pen and

notebook and stepped forward into the crowd entering the tattoo convention.

Twenty feet away, the world had been tourists in shorts holding the sweaty hands of their cranky children. But as Marion stepped into the murky light of the building, reality lurched into fantasy, a cave filled with surreal creatures, the air humid with the heat of bodies, reverberating with a bass beat, the scream of tattoo guns. A spider's red-and-black abdomen ballooned into view, its grasping, needle-sharp legs crawling across a shaded web of a forearm. A shower of stars fell across a shoulder; a bat, wings flung wide, flapped across a pale white back. Images swarmed over a man's naked torso and legs and arms, shrieking to a stop at hands, feet, face, which remained untouched, demure. Out of the corner of her eye, Marion saw another man, muscle and bone coming through his skin, so true to life she had to draw closer to check what she knew was not real. The man saw her fascination and smiled like a cat.

"Ready to feel some pain?" a skinny young man asked his friend as they walked by.

"It's been way too long," his friend replied.

Marion wandered between the rows of booths, feeling the music pulse against her skin, hearing the dentist-drill screech of the tattoo guns coming from all sides. A woman lay on her side on a padded table, her shirt drawn up and her pants unzipped and partially lowered to reveal the pale white of her stomach, the rise of her hip. Her arms stretched lazily above her head; her expression remained blank as the tattoo machine worked its way along the koi fish design that had been transferred to her skin. In the next booth an emaciated man grimaced each time the needles made contact, clenching his fist. Three teenagers watched him, nudging one another and pointing.

At the end of the aisle, in a corner booth, Marion caught sight of the back of a young woman, standing by one of the tables. The young woman removed her shirt and stood arguing with the heavily tattooed man holding a tattoo gun and someone who looked more official. The official handed her a surgical cover and she raised it to her chest and lay down on the table, exposing her right side. Marion could see the mound of a lush left breast underneath the cover. Where the right breast had been was simply a flat expanse, mowed across by a ragged, purple scar.

The woman looked up and caught Marion's eyes. She couldn't have been more than twenty-five years old, Marion thought.

"Assholes," the young woman said. "Told me I couldn't expose my breasts in public. 'Indecent exposure.' Can't put it out there if you don't have it, I told them."

Her eyes blazed in her thin face; her hair was short, spiked. She pointed to the two sides of her chest, one after another.

"Guess which one *they* think is indecent."

Marion's eyes filled. She had a sudden image of Kate after her surgery, her chest flat under the covers, her eyes huge and broken.

"You look like my mom," the woman on the tattoo table said to Marion. "What are you doing here?"

"I'm a journalist."

"Well, you can tell them all that I am getting a fucking victory tattoo. In public." She closed her eyes and put in her earphones, cranking the volume dial.

Marion moved across the last of the rooms of booths, walking through a field of conversations.

"That's the thing," an older man was saying insistently, "in the end, every piece we do gets buried or burned."

Two teenage girls lounged against a pillar.

"I'm going to get one the minute I turn eighteen," said one.

"Yeah. My mom says I can, but I've got to be able to cover it. Like, what's the point in that?"

As she walked outside the building she passed a man standing by the exit, a swirling seascape of waves flowing over his bare shoulders and down his back.

Years ago, when Marion's children were young, she took them to her mother's house in Iowa for a visit. Her children had been rambunctious, their bodies disrupted by the time change, their minds disjointed by the sudden shift in house rules, chasing one another about the house, flailing a long foam bat they had found in the hall closet. Marion walked into the living room, ready to tell them to take the bat outside, when the tip of the bat caught the edge of one of the family photographs on the wall and sent it flying. It landed on the couch, the children standing around it, openmouthed in shock.

Marion quickly picked up the picture, her fingers searching along the back for the wire. But she didn't feel the usual paper backing, the surface both too thick and too rough. She turned the frame over and saw an oil painting attached to the back, a seascape she recognized from years before when she used to watch her mother in her studio.

Hearing her mother coming, Marion swiftly hung the photograph back on the wall. But later at night, when her mother was asleep and Marion had finally convinced her children that they wouldn't fall out of the beds that were so foreign to them, she went back into the living room and worked her way around the space. Three, six, eight. Every photograph had a reverse side, a painting facing the wall.

"Want to go with me to the tattoo shop?" Marion sat in Daria's kitchen a week after the tattoo convention.

"Are you going to get inked, or are you going to watch?"

"I'm still working on the article," Marion said.

Daria buttered a piece of warm bread and handed it to Marion. "Don't you ever think it's funny?"

"What?"

"You got married, had kids, but a tattoo is too big of a commitment?"

"I'm going to do it; I promised Kate."

Daria looked at her sister, her face serious. "Hey, rule number one — never get a tattoo because someone else tells you to."

"Or because someone tells you not to?"

Daria started to reach toward the bait, but then sat back, thinking. Marion watched her, surprised; the Daria she knew always jumped into the argument, and Marion had been regretting her words even as they left her mouth. She would never have said them, she knew, if Daria's comment hadn't been so close to the truth.

"You know," Daria said, "when I got those first tattoos, Mom always said I did it because she'd told me I couldn't. But when I actually saw the designs on my skin, that wasn't what I was thinking about at all."

"What were you thinking?"

"That they were mine. And that they were beautiful."

Daria glanced down at the tattoos on her arm, an expression of almost maternal affection on her face. She looked up.

"You know, there is one thing you have to get used to, though."

Daria got up and went over to the catchall drawer of her kitchen. Marion always joked you could find anything in Daria's kitchen — playing cards, screwdrivers, old television remotes and unpaid car insurance bills.

Daria pulled out a bottle of bright purple nail polish. "Now, give me your hand."

"What?"

"Sweetheart, if you can't handle this, you'll never make it with a tattoo."

Marion watched the thick purple polish slide across her short, cropped fingernails. It had been twenty-five years since she and her daughter played spa in the backyard, Jeanne's small face intent as she painted water across her mother's nails. Jeanne had always insisted on real polish for her own nails, preferring greens and blues, sometimes orange, her fingers so small it took the merest touch of the brush to cover the surface. Jeanne would run around the house for hours after, her hands aloft in the air, making the colors swoop and weave like butterflies.

The house had always been full of sound and motion back in those days, the children's lives bouncing about the spaces like oversized beach balls. But Marion had loved the noise and activity, the way it pushed at the edges of her life, making it larger. She had loved the rampant chaos of toddler birthday parties, and even, although she rarely said so, the hormone-laden angst of her children's adolescent years, the way their bodies and emotions grew ahead of them, as if creating space for the adults they would become.

But then, as quickly as a simple breath in and out, the children had grown and gone, all the noises departing with them.

The day after she and Terry had taken their last child to college, Marion sat on the living room couch alone and listened to the house around her. It had been too many years to count since she had been in the house alone, without the knowledge that a child would be arriving soon. Sitting there on the couch, she thought with a small smile of all the sounds that would fill the house when they did return but at that moment, there was only the murmur of the refrigerator, the clunk of a neighbor's car door outside. Marion listened to the empty space around her. She could almost hear it moving, stretching out into the bedrooms, expanding into the area behind the couch where she used to hide the Christmas packages. It was the empty space that made her pay attention to the little clicks of the baseboard heater, the steady in and out of her own breath. Framed by stillness, the small sounds became art, worthy of contemplation once again.

"There," said Daria, sitting back and looking at her work. Marion's fingernails lay before them, ten small moments of gaudiness. "That should do it."

"*Now* will you come to the tattoo shop with me?"

"No." Daria grinned.

On the way home, Marion went to the grocery store, the ten moments of gaudiness taking Terry's favorite oatmeal from the shelf, sorting through packages of meat for the one with the longest expiration date, picking up a cantaloupe, a tomato, the purple bright against the red, pulling her mind away from the grocery store into images of color and shape, a memory of Jesse's triumphant three-year-old face above a handful of deep purple irises he had pulled out of the garden, the lilac fabric of a hot-air balloon they had taken once, on a whim, the children clinging to the basket, their hair aloft in the wind.

As she was picking up a head of lettuce, a young man stocking the shelves caught sight of her hands.

"Cool," he commented approvingly, before going back to stacking the carrots in a huge pyramid. A woman standing near him looked at Marion's nails, and then quickly away.

Marion went to the front of the store and picked a checkout clerk she knew, a normally disgruntled longtime employee. As Marion signed the credit card slip, the clerk saw her nails.

"Getting divorced?" The clerk's face was compassionate.

In the parking lot, a little girl stared at Marion and giggled; her mother followed her daughter's gaze.

"Grandchildren?" she said to Marion, with a conspiratorial wink.

Marion called Daria. "Why would you want to deal with that all the time?" she asked.

"*Now* you are starting to ask interesting questions," Daria replied.

Marion found an old bottle of nail polish remover. As the purple dissolved, her nails reappeared, quiet and pink, a crescent of white arcing across the top. When she finished, she put the cap back on the bottle, grabbed her purse and car keys and headed out to the local tattoo shop.

Marion's neighborhood was on the northwest side of the city, looking out over the water, set apart from the mainstream by both geography and culture. It had once been an enclave of Scandinavian fishermen, the houses small, the land swept clear of trees, as if any vegetation would inhibit the sight of the water from which the men gained their living. Stores had sold lutefisk and pastries that crumbled under your fingertips, leaving trails of hard, bright granules of sugar. Over time, the fishermen and their wives had grown older and a younger generation moved in, planting trees and tall condo buildings. Diners turned into French bistros. The Sunday farmer's market offered homemade soaps and knitted hats, and vegetables that used to be grown in backyards nearby.

The tattoo shop was one of the few hold-outs, along with the bar next door, the two inextricably grown together over the years. Marion didn't know how long the shop had been there; she remembered it from when they first moved in almost thirty years before, but it seemed like such an organic part of the landscape that it was hard to imagine the street ever being without it. A quietly simmering presence, squat and solid, curtains drawn at eye height — above them you could just catch glimpses of walls covered in white paper filled with lizards and stars and skulls. Marion had never been inside, although once the door had been open as she passed and she had seen a sign on the front desk: "We don't care what your cousin paid for his tattoo in Wichita."

Marion pulled up in front of the shop. The door was closed, but she could see pedestrians craning their heads as they passed, trying to look over the top of the curtains to catch sight of the designs on the wall, the people inside. Marion sometimes wondered who spent more time looking at tattoos — people with them or people without them — and then realized which camp she fell into.

The man behind the counter looked up as Marion walked in and gave a quick scan of her skin. She wished she had a tattoo to hold up, like an identification badge, an entry ticket.

"I'm writing an article," she began. She didn't expect excitement or even interest from the man in front of her. Some people were thrilled at the prospect of finding their way into print, a boost for their business, a possible photograph, but her assumption — correct, it appeared — was that that would not be the case here.

The man's hands were a crossword puzzle of words and letters; sailor and hula girls sashayed their way up his arms. Marion thought idly of the Green Stamps books her mother used to collect when Marion was a child, the prize you would get upon completion. This man must be almost there, she thought.

"I'm wondering if it would be okay if I talked to a few of the artists, watched a bit," she continued.

"I'll have to ask Kurt. He's in charge." The man didn't move.

"I don't care if she watches." The voice came from the corner of the room. Marion turned and saw an older woman, easily in her eighties, sitting in one of the plastic chairs lined up against the wall. She had a notebook in her lap, open to a design of an elaborate ship at sea.

"Are you getting that?" Marion walked over, intrigued.

"No, but it's fun to look. I'm getting this." She reached into her purse and pulled out a wedding ring, engraved with flowers and leaves. "I've worn it every day for the past sixty years. They had to cut it off me. Arthritis." She lifted up her curled hands, the knuckles large knobs. "I'm Bessie." She looked at Marion and smiled. "Who do you write for?"

"Magazines, newspapers. Stuff-of-life articles, mostly."

"Do you enjoy it?"

"It's good work."

"I always wanted to be a writer when I

was younger," Bessie said. "I suppose everybody says that, though, don't they?" She chuckled.

"What would you write about?" It surprised Marion to find herself asking that question. Normally, she would run as far as she could from stories of people's unrealized novels, their seven-hundred-page memoirs.

"Marmots," Bessie said without a moment's hesitation. "The way the snow melts, bit by bit, on Mount Rainier in the summer. I used to take my kids camping when they were little. I always wished there was a way to keep that feeling through the winter, you know, the way you would press a flower."

Bessie looked thoughtful for a moment and then turned to Marion.

"So, what would you write, if you could write anything?"

"Fiction," said Marion without thinking. "Stories."

"And why haven't you?" Bessie asked.

As the two women looked at each other, Kurt walked out from the back of the tattoo shop and called out Bessie's name.

Bessie sat at the tattoo station, Marion standing next to her while Kurt prepared needles and a palette of ink, his movements precise and automatic, part surgeon, part painter. He turned on the tattoo gun and the sound punctured the air.

"Are you sure, now?" Marion asked Bessie over the sound of the machine. "You can't take this back."

Kurt turned off the motor with a quick look of annoyance. Bessie turned to Marion, her eyes softening as she saw Marion's expression.

"Honey," Bessie said, "the clock runs faster than I do these days."

Point taken, Marion thought. She had never felt the simple urgency of time more than in the past few years, as her ovaries creaked into silence and she had gone for months and then a year without the gush of blood or the deep purple sadness that came with it. She had understood that something was ceasing within her and, more important, would never start again. The cold reality of it had struck her, as if, perched on the crest of a roller coaster, the rest of the ride was suddenly, irreversibly clear. On the way up, the vista had been infinite, the time to look about sometimes agonizingly long; now there was only the certain and dispassionate knowledge that there was one set of rails on which to travel, the ending immutable and about to begin. It didn't matter that the rest of the trip might take twenty, even thirty years to complete; the angle of the ride had changed.

She couldn't have told you whether the hot flashes came from the knowledge, or the knowledge brought them on. The heat would rise from within her, rolling out from the core of her being, cleaning out the brush of her life in its path — the unsaid things, good and bad, anger and frustration she had never expressed, flushed out of her along with the sweat that sprang to the surface of her skin.

As if to mirror the process going on inside, she had been overwhelmed with an almost desperate need to purify her life — plowing through the closets and shelves of her house, clearing out fashions she no longer cared about or fit into, books she never intended to read, odd condiments and dusty spices used once years ago. It was, in a strange way, like going back to the girl she had once been, who was strong and spare and didn't have things. Or maybe it was just that if you didn't have things, they couldn't be taken away.

And yet, she realized, sitting in the tattoo shop, the things she had held on to were the results of the irrevocable decisions in her life, the commitments she had leaped into without thought, with only the sure and perfect knowledge that it mattered not where her feet landed because her heart was certain. Standing at the altar with Terry, conceiving their children, she had felt a marvelous, liquid sense of clarity. Making those decisions had required rational thought only to determine when, but never if. She had known in her soul what she wanted and the only painful thing would have been not to move forward. It didn't matter what happened along the way, who changed or how. She knew.

So why couldn't she do it now? she wondered.

Bessie was looking at Marion as if she understood all of this and was amused by it, as if — and this Marion found ironic, given the line of her thought — Marion was somehow young and inexperienced.

"Tattoos are a little like wedding vows, aren't they?" Bessie said. "You grow up and change, even though the words you said don't. My husband always said you just have to believe in the future and be kind to the past."

"Ready now?" Kurt asked.

"But won't it hurt?" Marion looked at the crepe-thin surface of the woman's skin.

Bessie snorted. She sounded like Daria when she did that, Marion thought.

"I had six kids."

The tattoo man took Bessie's hand gently, like a courtier. She inclined her head in a nod and relinquished it to him. They leaned toward each other and the tattoo man placed the vibrating needles on the edge of the leaf design that had been transferred onto her finger.

Marion was making coffee the next morning when the phone rang.

"Mom?" her daughter's voice came across the lines, lit with excitement. "I'm going to have a baby!"

But you are a baby, Marion opened her mouth to say. I'm still holding you in my arms.

"You are the most beautiful, wonderful girl in the world," Marion said.

Jeanne's voice bubbled on, filled with stories. How quickly they had conceived, how ridiculously long it took for the narrow white stick to illuminate its plus sign, how Marion should come and stay for a month when the baby was born.

"We have a room all set up — for Dad, too, if he wants to come."

But all Marion could see was a dimly lit

hospital room, her daughter lying in the clear plastic bassinet just a few feet from her — a distance that had felt impossibly far, filled with cool and weightless air, without the pulse of blood, a heart. Marion remembered carefully maneuvering herself out of bed and walking over to her child, lifting up the small body, bundled like a loaf of bread, and bringing her back to bed where she curled in the curve of Marion's arm.

"You'll come, won't you?" Jeanne's voice was suddenly unsure.

"With cameras and baby clothes and so much advice you'll be kicking us out by the end of the first week," Marion promised.

Marion had been twenty-six when she realized she was pregnant for the first time. She remembered lying next to Terry, drowsy and relaxed after hours of loving exploration, hearing the sounds of her husband's breath moving in and out with sleep. And suddenly, she had known. As if someone had walked into the room and spoken to her, she knew she was not alone in her body anymore and, in some ways, never would be again. For even after the children were born, it seemed as if they instantly started creating memories and associations, as if, no longer sharing a body, they were weaving the ties that would hold them to each other, wind them into each other's hearts.

And now, twenty-eight years later, her daughter was pregnant.

There were moments in life, Marion thought, when you reached back, baton in hand, feeling the runner behind you. Felt the clasp of their fingers resonating through the wood, the release of your hand, which then flew forward, empty, into the space ahead of you.

"How's the tattoo research going?" Terry asked Marion as they walked through the gardening section at the giant hardware store. It was Saturday; the celebration of their daughter's pregnancy had quieted to an underlying hum of joy in their lives. Terry needed to pick up some plumbing supplies — the upstairs toilet was leaking again — and Marion had promised Hadley they would use Terry's truck to pick up some extra large bags of mulch for Hadley's garden.

Marion told Terry about the old woman and her wedding ring tattoo. "She never even flinched," Marion said. "And I don't think she'll ever have second thoughts."

"You know, sweetheart," Terry said,

"you're the kind of person who wouldn't think twice if someone said you needed to get a tattoo for me or the kids. Doing it for you, though, that might be a trick."

They hefted a bag of mulch and tossed it onto the cart.

"I think maybe you need a little inspiration," Terry remarked, straightening up and looking around.

"How about that one?" He pointed down the aisle to a young woman, the head of a dragon emerging from the edge of her tank top, its tongue long and forked, its eyes wild. "You'd look exotic, don't you think?" He traced the lines lightly on Marion's shoulder.

Marion felt the tip of his finger moving in careless curves, traveling lazily from the top of her shoulder down the soft skin on the back of her arm.

"How about his?" she challenged, pointing to the red-and-orange flames that meandered up the neck of the young woman's boyfriend. Marion ran her fingers gently from the edge of Terry's collar up into his hair.

"I always liked tattoos here," Terry said casually, bringing her wrist up to his mouth. His lips lingered against her skin.

"Look how short that checkout line is,"

Marion commented. "We could be home in no time."

Marion sat in front of her computer, smiling slightly to herself. Soon she would go and start dinner, but now, sitting at her desk, the world and she felt quiet, whole.

The plumbing supplies were still in the truck, the toilet unfixed. Marion ran her index finger down the bones of her left hand, over the veins that were starting to raise and make themselves known. She remembered the first time she had looked down and thought, Someday these will be my grandmother's hands. But for now, she thought of Terry, how their fingers had drifted across each other in the course of their long, slow afternoon, lingering on the softness under his chin, of her belly, the gray in his hair, the ripples of the varicose vein that climbed up the back of her left leg — the same way they had, as young lovers, touched breasts, the long sweet curve of a hip, turning their bodies into liquid gold.

She knew she should be writing notes for her article, but instead she found herself looking out the window, her eye catching on the black stone that rested on the sill. Into her imagination came the image of a young boy at the edge of an ocean, a stone in his hand — his mother standing a few yards behind him, watching her son, her face full of love and confusion. Marion wondered who they were and how they had come into her mind, what that moment in their lives meant. She wanted to follow it, follow them, as if they were a trail. She opened her computer and began to write.

It was the greatest adventure she could imagine, this fictional world of people she had never met, the way their lives unfurled into her mind and out her fingers, onto the page. Over the next few weeks, she found herself waking before dawn, in mid-conversation with the characters who resided so comfortably in her dreams, and she would slip out of bed and rush to her computer, to place them somewhere solid and tangible so she would be able to find them again when the sun came up and the world was practical and imaginations were best used to figure out how to turn yesterday's leftovers into today's dinner.

Over the weeks, in her mind, on the page, the boy grew into a man, his relationship with his mother raveling and unraveling. She learned quickly not to push the characters down roads they didn't want to walk, to let them choose their own pasts; she was glad only for the chance to listen. She hadn't had imaginary friends as a child, and certainly not during the time when anyone would have considered her a grown-up.

Maybe this is my midlife crisis, she thought, amused. My little red sports car of words.

But she didn't care. The deadline for the tattoo article passed and she took no new assignments.

"I've got family in town," she said by way of explanation.

At the end of each day, she would print out the pages she had written, the pile rising like a staircase until one day all that was left was to open the door at the top and let the characters out into the world.

"Will you read it?" Marion asked, holding out the stack of pages to Daria.

When she left Daria's house, Marion drove to the tattoo shop.

"Ready?" asked Kurt as they sat down on either side of the table.

"Ready," Marion said.

Marion held out her hand; Kurt turned her wrist so the skin on the underside faced toward him.

"What shall we write?" he asked.

AVA

The other women had been angry with Ava for not being there during Kate's illness, the implication heavy in their voices — but you've done cancer; you should be there, you know what to do. As if death was a marketable skill, Ava thought, an experience you got better at and could put on your résumé: "Does death well." Well, of course yes, she did, she had and they all knew it. By the age of ten, she had learned how to be the guard dog, standing at the door of her mother's hospital room to keep out the visitors who couldn't handle disease — the ones with the tight eyes and the too-big bouquets of flowers, the ones who would eventually spurt out some comment about their own terrible day, about the slight of a salesperson, a twinge in the ankle that made it impossible to run five miles that morning. The ones who came to her mother, their pre-mourning hanging on them like designer shrouds, off-loading their grief onto a woman already sinking into the bed. She had learned how nervousness derailed some people's words, how fear blinkered their vision, and when she saw those visitors coming she would quickly step outside and close the door behind her, inform them that her mother was sleeping, would likely be sleeping for some time.

It had been during those weeks in the hospital, while Ava's father was at work, that Ava and her mother started playing gin rummy, laying the cards out across the top of the swing-armed table that rotated into position over her mother's bed. Perhaps it was the long games, or the visitors, or the endlessly revolving door of hope and exhaustion that was her mother's existence, but Ava had found herself developing a personal theory she called the Card Game of Life. In that game, dying people trumped everything. They won — whatever food or music or flowers or voices on the phone they wanted, they got. They won if your day was lousy, if you failed a test, if you were terrified by the sight of your mother's face falling into itself. You dealt with that yourself because you weren't sick; you didn't trump. It seemed only fair, as they were losing everything else, for them to win at something.

There was a clarity to the rules that was utterly missing in a hospital room where everything was hypothetical, experimental, riveted to reality only by pain. It was only years later that Ava realized that the rules of the Card Game of Life, while blessedly clear-cut, were impossible to sustain because the players were people, themselves experimental creatures, held to reality by pain and love, their tolerance of which varied considerably.

But Ava didn't know that back then. So she taught herself how not to inhale, when every breath told her that the scent of her mother had changed, lost its clarity, the essence of cinnamon and fall leaves that Ava had loved now damp and moldy, emitting a smell that Ava knew wasn't going away, would only get worse, even when the doctors tried to tell her and her father about new treatments, lots of hope. She knew. Spending all that time at the hospital, her nose had become adept at recognizing death while it was still weeks away. She'd known about the man down the hall; she had sensed the change as she walked by his room, an odor like dust and cheese, with an underlying note of a brick basement in the summer. One time she thought she could smell it on a woman who was visiting a patient. She wondered if she should tell the woman, but what could you do? No one would believe you.

And then there was Kate — so many years later, but fear and sorrow are like perfume, Ava had realized. You might lose the top and middle notes over time, but the base note always stays, ready to throw you back to where you started. What was she supposed to say when people looked at her and shook their heads, reminded her of how long she had known Kate, disappointment and disapproval woven through their words. What could she say? That the possibility of the smell of death on her best friend was more than she could stand? That she didn't know if she could play the game again, keep her face neutral, be supportive, if her nose told her things the doctor would not?

"I'm busy," she would say, "work is crazy. I can't fly up now." And she would spend her nights trying to imagine a scent that was Kate — caring and thoughtful, with a small smile in the middle notes. A scent to remind Kate of herself if she started to get lost. Except, miraculously, Kate didn't get lost, and Ava was left feeling as if she held a handful of cards with nowhere to put them.

■ ■ ■ ■

So on the night of Kate's victory party, when Kate told Ava that her challenge was to do the breast cancer fund-raising walk — three days, sixty miles — Ava accepted the satisfaction in the other women's eyes, even as she couldn't meet Kate's.

When Ava was a child, back when her mother baked enchiladas and dug in the garden, Ava had loved the power of her own nose. She had delighted in how she could tell, without even looking, who was entering a room and where they had been that day. She knew if her father had gone to a Mexican restaurant on his lunch break or grabbed a hot dog from the stand outside his office building, knew when she hugged her mother after school if she had visited their next-door neighbor, who washed all her beautiful cashmere and silk by hand in Woolite, the whispery floral scents so pink and blue Ava could almost see the stripes on the bottle when she inhaled. She could tell if a guest in their house had passed the building where the newspaper was printed, or leaned over to breathe in the roses that her mother grew along the walkway to their house. She looked at people and thought about how they spent their lives traveling through the world, collecting scents they weren't even aware of and leaving their own behind, creating a trail a child could follow. It made her feel safe to know where the people around her had been, to know that they carried their lives on their skin, a story for her to read.

A teacher had once explained to Ava that there were no smells in outer space; they needed gravity to exist. Ava understood, although after her mother died, for her it was the reverse. In her post-mother world, all there was was gravity, indiscriminately pulling everything — light, smell, taste, touch, sound — down to the flat, hard earth, below which was her mother. There was nothing above.

Everyone had tried to reach her — her father, the neighbor next door, her favorite teacher who had always greeted her in the morning with a scent of lavender and oatmeal, but who now smelled like nothing. The summer after Ava's mother died, Ava's father took her to Lopez Island where their cabin was a shortcut through the woods from Kate's family's cottage. From the time Ava was three, summers had meant Lopez Island and Kate, the two girls walking on the rocky beaches together, diving off the platform into water so cold that only children and old men seemed able to tolerate it. Kate had spent the summer after Ava's mother died shoving things under Ava's nose — crab shells and blackberries, seaweed and sap from a pine tree.

"Come on, Sleeping Beauty," Kate would urge. "Wake up."

But the world had stayed gray, for years. It was easier that way. If you didn't smell the sulfur of the match, you wouldn't think about how it wasn't your mother lighting the birthday candle. If you didn't smell Elmer's glue, you wouldn't remember all the Valentine's and Christmas cards she had insisted you make — you pouting, she insistent — "Give to those you love, Ava," she would say, and now it only made you realize you couldn't.

It wasn't until after high school that things really changed. The upscale department store nearby was hiring the summer before Ava and Kate started college and they decided that, having spent all their summers together in the past, they should work together as well. Kate got a job in the shoe department, chasing small children who would rather run than be fitted for shoes.

Ava lobbied for a position in cosmetics, but she ended up next door in perfume.

"Lucky stiff," Kate commented, coming off the end of her shift, wiping bits of granola bar from her hair.

At first, Ava had approached her job as a good if uninspired foot soldier, spraying samples on thin, pointed strips of white paper, waving them three times to disperse the top notes before handing them to customers and dutifully ringing up and wrapping their purchases. No opinions, no comments, the perfumes passing by, mute as car parts on an assembly line.

It was the woman with the auburn hair who changed things. Ava had seen her before, lean and graceful, running her shining red Irish setter around the lake, the two of them mirror images of each other. But here the woman stood in front of Ava at the department store counter, holding a giant white poodle of a perfume, the essence of roses and lilacs thick in the bottle in her hand.

Why was it, thought Ava, suppressing a sudden surge of irritation, that people could so effortlessly, unintentionally, choose dogs that looked exactly like them, and yet be so inept when selecting a scent that would be welcomed by their own skin? How many gentle, kind men had passed her wearing a bullhorn message of musk and engine oil; how many strong, beautiful women had come to her counter swaddled in the essence of talcum powder or lost in a forest of sandalwood?

"No," Ava had said, taking the bottle from the woman with the auburn hair standing in front of her. "Not that one."

"What?" The woman looked up in surprise.

"That's not you."

"What do you mean?" The woman seemed intrigued rather than annoyed, which helped.

"You aren't flowers." Ava started off tentatively, but then gathered assurance. "You are golds and oranges, not purples and pink." When the woman looked a little confused, Ava instinctively grabbed a bottle from behind her.

"Smell this." Ava sprayed the perfume, not on the tester strip but on the woman's left wrist. "You want it on the arm that's nearest your heart, where it's warmest. Now wait a minute for the top notes to pull back before you smell." The assurance in her voice startled her. When was the last time she had felt that confident?

They stood, the scent in the air about

them evoking images of red maple trees, yellow-tinged bamboo, a whisper of black tea floating through rice-paper walls. Ava watched as the woman's shoulders relaxed.

"Yes," she said simply, raising her wrist to her face.

"You should let it interact with your skin a bit before you make your decision."

"I already know," the woman said.

As Ava rang up the purchase, she could smell the perfume settling into the woman in front of her, becoming a part of her.

"Thank you," the woman said, resting her left hand for just a moment on Ava's shoulder. Ava breathed in, cinnamon and fall leaves, and felt her nose awaken.

After that, Ava could feel the awful weight of gravity lessening, inhalation by inhalation, each breath increasing the space between earth and sky, colors and tastes and thoughts slipping in along with the smells, as loving and longed for as old friends walking into her arms. She found herself stopping on the porch in the mornings when the air was straight off the lake, fresh and cool and green, to breathe in slowly and gratefully. As she rode the bus home at the end of her workday, she found herself noticing the perfumes about her — how some created a small quiet oasis around their people and others were more aggressive, jostling against one another like elbows, claiming territory. Sometimes she would sense a perfume from one side of the bus reaching toward another, mingling, the wearers unknowing, looking out their respective windows, and she would spend her bus ride wondering what it would take for them to turn around and see each other.

At work she became bolder with her opinions, her confidence reinforced each time she saw a scent nestle into the skin of its wearer, whose eyes would widen in recognition. Her growing reputation for matching clients to scents traveled through the department store with an efficiency usually reserved for gossip regarding upper management.

"It's getting a little ridiculous," Kate commented. "I overheard the women in Evening Wear calling you the Perfume Whisperer." But Kate didn't mind, wasn't sad that there was no equivalent title for her in the shoe department; she was happy to see her friend emerging from the sterile world in which she had submerged herself. The new Ava swam in her rediscovered sense of smell with relief and joy, and it was all Kate could do to stop her from accosting people on the street and offering suggestions on how to improve their olfactory reality.

Ava and Kate went to the local university together that fall, Kate studying economics and public relations, while Ava bush-whacked her way through the bureaucratic system to create her own major — a combination of history, literature, biology and chemistry that she called simply Sensing Smell. Her studies made her an interesting, if occasionally annoying, roommate.

"Did you know," Ava would say, looking up from her book, "that measles smell like plucked chicken feathers?"

"Thank you for that," Kate answered steadily from her chosen position at the kitchen table. "I'm sure I'll find that information helpful in my career."

But in fact, for Ava it all was. When she left college it was to work with a perfume atelier in Los Angeles, where she quickly gained a following among the more powerful figures in the business and entertainment industry. There was the curly-haired method actor who wanted a cologne to help him inhabit the role of the moment; the museum curator looking to tint exhibit brochures with the fragrance of leather and stewing apples of seventeenth-century

Jamestown or the sunflowers of southern France; the best-selling romance author who wanted different smells — sometimes perfume but more often simple domestic scents like cut apples or Emmental cheese — to evoke the characters in the book she was currently writing; the professional wife who would bring in a shirt from the man she wanted to marry next and have Ava select a perfume for her that would complement his smell.

Ava's clients could instinctively recognize a match between a fragrance and a person or place when it was presented to them, that elusive connection, the subliminal joining of scent and soul; they could see the effect the right fragrance had on others (Ava always smiled at how the slightest hint of vanilla and chocolate, that faint hope of home-baked cookies, had helped tip a board's decision to hire one of her clients as the CEO of the major home decor chain). But her clients could not create the match themselves, which made Ava's career choice a lucrative one. And while she had the occasional Seattle client, it was in Los Angeles, with its twin idols of money and all things feng shui, that her job security was guaranteed.

■ ■ ■ ■

It had been Ava's idea to promote the concept of perfume parties as a way to expand the reach of the store beyond its location. By that point, Ava had lived in Los Angeles for almost ten years and she and Monica, the store's owner, had become business partners. Business was steady but repetitive, for all that the cast of characters who entered the store were themselves flamboyant, famous or simply wanting to be. Ava found herself knowing their scents even before they opened the door. It was all too easy, like a juggler using only one pin; she wanted more in her hands.

And so, for an initially modest, and then — as the idea of perfume parties became popular, written up in local and then national magazines — an exorbitant fee, she would go to gatherings at corporations, mansions, clothing store openings with her specially made leather case. Fifty one-ounce bottles arranged on shelves lined with cream-colored silk. She felt like a magician each time she opened the case to the sound of collective, covetous sighs. Over the years she had learned, like any good artist, to make sure the lighting was angled to reflect off the edges of the bottles, the gold and clear and pink liquids within, had learned to open the case slowly so there was no apprehension about spillage, only rising expectation.

Over the years of doing parties, she had realized the events were more successful if she let her clients explore the fragrances first, opening and inhaling one after another until finally they became overwhelmed and turned to her. She discovered a great deal watching them during that time — noting the ones who lingered over each bottle in conversation with the scent within, the ones who moved quickly from perfume to perfume on a single-minded quest for their match, like tourists racing through the Louvre wanting only to find the *Mona Lisa*. As she observed the gesture of a hand, the pitch of a voice, she was already making preliminary matches of her own.

Afterward she would sit down with them one at a time and ask them questions: where had they grown up, what foods would they eat late at night, where did they relax — beach, mountains, cities, bed — what books had reached into their souls? As they talked, she smelled salt water, biscuits, juniper, ginger, wood smoke, a blanket fresh from the dryer, dark chocolate, cherry blossoms, dried edelweiss held between the pages of a childhood paperback. As she asked her clients about their lives, she watched them relax and become expansive, their initial responses like top notes, designed for quick inhalation, leading to more reflective insights under the warmth of her attention. Ava learned to wait for the base note; it would tell her what she needed most to know. Usually it was something hidden — a sorrow, a joy, an anger or a desire to be kind. Beneath all the day-to-day maneuverings of a personality, the base note remained constant, a color upon which all the others rested but which was rarely acknowledged or perceived. Without all the layers, a perfume match was at best superficial, a name tag rather than an intimate conversation.

One evening in June, Ava packed her case, making sure each bottle was full, and set out for an event in Pasadena. Ava lived some twenty minutes away, in a small house she had bought years before in a somewhat questionable neighborhood, avoiding the clean and sterile high-rises she might have afforded. But she had loved the fragrance palette of her street, the scent of corn tortillas and frying oil and meat that greeted her as she turned the corner, how the smell turned into garlic and oregano and fennel as she continued up the hill, changing if she went past her house into strawberries and red wine, chanterelle mushrooms in warm butter and sherry. At the top she could smell the crisp silver scent of eucalyptus. Her hill and the winding road that led up it was an olfactory microcosm of the city she lived in, always in transition, reflecting her own feeling that she had never quite unpacked her last box, as if that made leaving an easier proposition.

She had tried to put her roots down in Los Angeles; she had bought her house and painted its walls in rich terra-cottas and sage greens, filled the rooms with the scents of cumin and coriander, fresh-cut oranges and papaya and banana. There had been men over the years, the sharp marine smells of their shampoos and the muskier fragrance of their clothes, the unsweetened mint toothpaste of the outdoorsman, the shoe polish of the investment broker. The men had stayed for longer or shorter periods of time, but they always left or were asked to. For Ava, everything — even or perhaps particularly men — was its smell. She had been part of a study when she was in college, testing human sensitivity to olfactory stimuli; whether good or bad, after fifteen minutes most of the participants no longer were aware of a scent. Olfactory accustomization was a human survival trait, the study determined. Unfortunately for Ava, it seemed to work against the concept of long-term relationships; she couldn't love what she could no longer smell.

The one constant in her life over the years had been Kate. Kate was the one Ava called when she broke up with her first boyfriend in LA, when she thought she was pregnant with the man who showed up too quickly after that, when she was choosing colors for her house, when her perfume parties got a two-page spread in a big fashion magazine. In the larger picture of Ava's life, Kate was summer at the cabin, a long, open stretch of time to remember who you were. And when Kate got sick, Ava was as far from the cabin as she could get, for once glad of her remote location.

So Ava felt she deserved the challenge of the fund-raising walk that Kate had handed her, and the physical commitment it required was daunting enough that it seemed like a proper penance. Ava had trained steadily since Kate had given her the challenge, determined to succeed in what she saw as an understudy position, having failed utterly at a leading role in Kate's illness. It was not going to be easy, unlike — she thought with a flash of irritation — making bread. Ava's desire to be surrounded by only the most fascinating of culinary fragrances had kept her slim, but with the exception of an ill-fated stint of rock climbing with the outdoorsman, sweat had not been a perfume in her collection in the decades since she had moved to Los Angeles.

She had begun training for the walk on a treadmill in a gym, resigned to, even desiring the monotony of being within four walls, but over the months, as two miles had grown to three and four and five, so did her boredom with the endless fragrance loop of chlorine and sweat and expensive herbal shampoos, and she had turned to the hills behind her house, where a curiosity to find the epicenter of an elusive smell often overcame any tiredness in her legs. Over the months, as her muscles and lungs became stronger, she had tracked the aroma of chocolate cake to a child's birthday party, discovered a group of engineering graduate students brewing beer in their garage, a neighborhood chili cook-off, complete with motorized bucking bronco. Yet even as she collected the scents in her memory, she felt as if she was waiting for something she hadn't yet smelled.

She found the address for the party in Pasadena and got out of her car, perfume case in hand, ready for her last event before summer, when people would travel and spend their days inhaling new and invigorating smells. They would come back to her in the fall, when their jobs took them indoors again and they would find themselves missing something they couldn't quite describe. But for a few months, summer would do Ava's job for her.

The demarcation line for summer in Los Angeles, where the seasons came at you sunny and bland, indistinguishable as Twinkies rolling off a conveyor belt, was less obvious than in Seattle and in many ways had more to do with calendar than climate. Even after more than twenty years in LA, Ava had a hard time getting used to it. Particularly now, when the spring rains would be soaking the Northwest, pulling the tulips out of the ground, spotlighting the bright whites and pinks of magnolia and dogwood blossoms, she missed the liquid silver of her hometown and the sweet smell of daphne blossoms even as she enjoyed the fact that as she knocked on the door of the

Pasadena home her legs were bare under her skirt.

Despite the somewhat formidable aspect of the house's white columns and circular drive, the group inside the Pasadena house was warm and welcoming. Four generations gathered together to celebrate the ninety-second birthday of their matriarch, a woman with hands curled by age but whose eyes caught every current in the room. Her scent would be easy, Ava knew immediately — the smell of beach grass and sun-dried laundry; underneath, the sharp, bright smell of typewriter ribbons. Her daughter was milk and vanilla, all rounded edges and open arms, the hostess of the party, of course. Add just a bit of white musk and tobacco and it would be the scent she would hide in the back of her drawer, visit but never wear. The youngest girl, a tall, lithe thing of ten years or so, was evergreens and beach rocks. Thoughts of Lopez Island and Kate washed over Ava whenever the girl was near.

But it was the girl's mother whom Ava could not decipher. The woman stayed at the edge of the party, despite the best efforts of her daughter and mother to pull her in with food or conversation. Ava watched as the daughter brought her mother bottle after small bottle of perfume for her to smell, noticed how the mother nodded, smiled, but never breathed in the scent. When it came time for matching, she was the last to come into the small side room where Ava was conducting individual sessions. Her answers to Ava's questions were bland and monochromatic, devoid of olfactory details or colorings. All the same, Ava could not dismiss the feeling that she had never met anyone more alert to the sensation of smell. The woman sat, rigid as a hunting dog, her focus complete to the point that it seemed to block any other scent but the one she had been born to detect. In the room alone with Ava — without the need for a certain level of politeness that had obviously been bred into her — discussions of food, locations and childhood memories were all tossed aside with a certain visceral impatience.

At the end of her questions, with no solid clues on which to rely, Ava remarked almost offhandedly that she was often in the presence of women at her gatherings, but rarely were they all related to one another. How interesting it was, how feminine the family seemed to be.

The woman looked at her with an expression of such angry and unfiltered grief that Ava recoiled instinctively. She was not known for social gaffes; usually her sense of smell was more accurate. Jealousy, nervousness, pride, lust were all scents her nose easily detected, allowing her to reroute a conversation accordingly.

"I'm sorry," Ava said. "Whatever it is, I didn't know."

Ava waited. The smell of sorrow in the room was so strong it obliterated all other scents. Without them, Ava had no sense of where to go.

"My son," the woman said, her voice flat. "He drowned, two summers ago. He was ten."

The woman looked around the room. "After he died, I could still smell him in his room. But one day they convinced me to go out, and when I came back, they had taken all his things away. They said it wasn't healthy. They told me to remember my daughter." The woman looked at Ava and the case of perfume bottles by her side. "I want my son."

And Ava knew that no matter what scents she put together, she could not bring this woman back into the world when the only thing she wanted was what wasn't in it anymore.

"I'm so sorry for your loss." Her hands empty.

As she left the party, Ava passed the mother's daughter and the scent of evergreens followed Ava into her car.

Ava drove back to the perfume store and found her business partner sitting in her office, surrounded by piles of scarves from France.

"They have just that bit of fragrance, you know?" Monica said as Ava walked in. "Just a moment of walking along the Seine, that half-second before you enter the Louvre."

"Monica," Ava said, "I need to go home."

Any concern that she might be doing the wrong thing evaporated as Ava looked out of the airplane window and saw Seattle, silver and blue and deeply green, the lines of the water and islands that surrounded the city curving open in welcome, curling into safe places to go and figure out your life. It always surprised her, the amount of green, the uninhabited blue, after living in a city where houses steamrolled their way over hills and mountains and deserts, leaned off cliffs and put their feet in the ocean.

It hadn't been easy, convincing Monica. They had finally settled on a three-month sabbatical when it appeared that Ava was adamant.

"It's just a minor midlife crisis," Monica — who knew what she was talking about — had said. "You're efficient. Three months should be plenty."

Now, on the plane home, Ava inhaled in anticipation and caught a flash of excitement from the little girl sitting next to her.

"I'm going home," the little girl told her, leaning over Ava's lap to look out the window. "I've been with my dad; now I'm going back to my mom."

The little girl looked at Ava, curious. "Where are you going?"

"To Lopez Island, to smell the blackberries."

"My mom says the blackberries won't be ready for a while."

"I don't mind waiting," Ava replied.

The cabin was as she remembered it; her father had taken care over the years to preserve it the way it had been when Ava was a child. The same red-and-white-striped dish towels, the ancient fold-out couch that left guests creaking in the morning, the cot on the screened-in porch that she had loved to sleep in when she was small, feeling the excitement of being alone out in the world, yet still safe within the enclosure of her family. Even after her mother died and Ava refused to sleep on the porch anymore, her father had kept the bed there. Just in case, he always said. You never know when you might want an adventure.

She put down the bag of groceries her father had thrust upon her when she stopped by his house in Seattle on the way to the island.

"I know you want to be there by yourself for a little while," he had said. "But feel free to call your dad if you want company."

As she unloaded the groceries, Ava smiled. Her father knew her temptations — fine-ground coffee, Mexican chocolate, a bottle of single-malt scotch. She opened the bag of coffee, cracked the seal on the bottle, and inhaled slowly and deeply.

Lopez was one of the flatter of the San Juan Islands, known mostly as farmland, its landscape rolling rather than peaked. Walking the long, flat roads that circled the island, Ava was often passed by bicyclists and cars loaded down with camping gear. The locals were friendly, waving and offering rides. If they'd heard what she was training for they usually stopped and told her stories. It seemed everyone knew someone, their words spilling out on the road, the smell of their sadness or anger or acceptance overtaking the air until she would make excuses, comment on cooling muscles, a need to finish ten miles that day, to keep on schedule.

In the late afternoon, she would walk the beach in front of the cabin. There was space for her thoughts on its long expanse and she found them traveling, wandering across the water. The waves sputtered up across the rocks; her feet crunched on the sand and pebbles below her. She played a game she used to play with Kate as a child, looking for rocks that would reflect the mood of the day. Round speckled ones, a glowing orange oval, wet from the sea. At the end of the day, she would bring her favorite back to the cabin and add it to the collection on the fireplace mantel, a long line of stones, beginning with the one Kate had given her the night of the victory party.

In the evenings Ava would make dinner — salads with pale orange carrots, basil and giant tomatoes from the farmer's market, fish from the local marina. She would take her plate out to the porch and watch the sun start to think about setting. She would salute its final leave-taking around ten in the evening with a glass of scotch as she listened to the world grow quiet, the flowers closing, the fragrance of the warm air rising off the surface of the land and mingling with the soft peat smell in the glass in her hand.

It surprised her not to be lonely or to miss the perfume parties and the interplay between customer and fragrance. Instead, she found herself paying attention to the smells of the landscape around her in a new and different way, fascinated by how the mist on cooler mornings brought out the sharp snap of pine trees, how the sun pulled the scent of dried grass from the lawn. In Los Angeles, her ability to bring out the essence of each individual through a perfume was a gift few could match; here she was simply doing what nature had always done. It surprised her, too, how little that bothered her.

One afternoon in the middle of August, from the woods bordering the overgrown lawn that stretched from the cabin down to the beach, Ava heard the old eagle whistle Kate had spent months perfecting the summer they were nine. She looked over and saw Kate, heading toward her.

"Your dad told me you were here," Kate called out when she got closer. "I thought you might want a walking partner."

■ ■ ■ ■

Ava and Kate sat at an outside table at Kate's favorite Lopez restaurant, looking out to the water. They had walked twelve miles that day, Ava watching for any sign of fatigue on Kate's part. Kate had laughed it off.

"You're not the only one doing something challenging this summer," she had reminded Ava. "I've been in training, too."

They had arrived at the restaurant around seven and by the time they had finished their dinner and were drinking the last of their wine, the sun was setting and the air starting to cool.

"So, how are you feeling these days about rafting the Grand Canyon?" Ava asked.

"Scared." Kate's mood dipped.

"How so?"

"Well . . ." Kate took a sip of wine. "It's not the rapids — I mean, it is, but it isn't. It just feels like such a risk.

"I understand that's the point," Kate continued. "But here's the thing I keep thinking about — a risk is a risk *because* it's avoidable. We've both done unavoidable, and it's horrible. But if something happens in the Grand Canyon, it will be a loss that didn't have to happen. I don't know what to do with that anymore."

Ava nodded. "But it happens anyway," she said. "I didn't come when you were sick because I was scared I might see you die. I couldn't risk it. A lot of good that did me — it's gonna take a whole bunch of walking to get back to where I was."

"Is that why you think I gave you the 3-Day Walk, to punish you?"

Ava looked at Kate and nodded.

Kate shifted her gaze out over the water. "You know," she said, after a time, "they say you can never know what cancer will bring out in someone. I remember one time, I was sitting in the waiting room at the hospital before my chemo session and a delivery man came in. He was so alive — you could just feel it. I wanted what he had so badly. At that moment, I would've given my cancer to him, if I could have. Even knowing what that meant, knowing what I would've been doing to another human being, I'd have given it to him; I was just so tired." She paused. "You don't know what you'll do, Ava. Nobody does. And I can't judge."

"You're not angry with me?"

"I didn't say that," Kate answered with a wry smile. "But it's not why I gave you that challenge."

"Then why?"

A maze of emotions flickered across Kate's face and then she raised her glass.

"I wanted you to come home," she said simply.

At 5:30 A.M. on the first day of the 3-Day Walk, Kate drove Ava to the starting point at the university parking lot.

"Wow," said Ava, as they inched their way forward in a line of cars that stretched out of the campus and down the road. Some of the walkers, forgoing the wait, had hopped out of vehicles and were heading up the road wearing backpacks adorned with pink flags. Ava saw team signs and T-shirts — the Mammogrammys, Walkers for Knockers, Save Second Base. There were enlarged photographs of women — healthy, turbaned, with children — with birth and death dates underneath. One woman wore a shirt that read simply: "I Walk for My Dad." When Ava and Kate finally pulled up to the front of the line they saw twenty-five huge white trucks, an elaborate series of tents, a stage with blaring music, and thousands of people, hugging, crying, jumping up and down to keep themselves warm in the cool morning air. It was like some strange funereal carnival. In pink.

"Are you going to be okay?" Kate asked. "I didn't know it was going to be quite like this."

"Sure," said Ava, pulling out a pair of dark glasses.

Twenty miles later, Ava trudged into camp at four in the afternoon, exhilarated and exhausted, the muscles of her legs twitching. She went to the storage truck, grabbed her backpack and headed for the assigned number of her campsite. While she knew the walk wasn't a race, she was pleased to see how few tents were already pitched — jaunty little pink outposts in the midst of a vast frontier. It was a little like the Oklahoma land rush, only with better bras. Ava wondered, not for the first time that day, who her tent-mate would be. Although Ava had resisted the idea of joining a team, of spending all that time with women upending the secrets of their lives into your ears while their perfumes were telling you exactly the opposite, the downside of not being part of a team was that you didn't know whom you would be sleeping with. It was unlikely to be a beautiful man.

She walked down the aisle of numbers, looking for E-35. Sitting in front of a neat, pink tent was a white-haired woman Ava had seen throughout the day. There were plenty of older women on the walk, much to Ava's surprise, as she thought the walk was rigorous even for a young person, but this woman was the kind you noticed — with gloriously white hair framing a face with naturally smooth skin and cheekbones that could hold back a hurricane. But mostly it was her expression, the compassion on her face when Ava had spotted her talking with various people throughout the day. And she seemed to talk to anyone — the crew member handing out sports bars, the twin walking for her sister, the overweight woman who was sitting dejected at the pit stop, the team of young people who had made a running detour into a Dairy Queen and then shared their ice cream with her when she had laughingly stepped to the side to give them a place back in the line of walkers.

Ava approached and the older woman looked up, smiling.

"Hi," she said. "Are you in E-thirty-five?"

Ava nodded.

"Well, I'm Elaine, and you're just in time for mimosas."

Ava looked at the woman's raised hand holding a slim, sparkling plastic glass, and smiled.

"That's the best thing I've heard all day," she said, and dropped the weight of her pack to the ground.

Ava sipped her mimosa, marveling at Elaine, who seemed ready to make a celebration out of anything. The only other person she'd ever known like that was Kate, the Queen of the Lopez Island Tea Party, as her father had called her. When they were young, Kate could spend hours making plates out of salal leaves, begging chipped teacups and cookies from her mother. And here was Elaine, fresh from the showers, wearing a Hawaiian batik sundress and rubbing peppermint lotion into her feet.

"I've found it's the little things that make the walk better," she commented.

"How many times have you done this?" Ava asked.

"This is my third walk. I started the year my daughter died."

"I'm so sorry; I should have thought."

"But that's why we're here, isn't it? Even those peppy little teamsters over there" — Elaine pointed to the group of boisterous twenty-somethings whose effortless stamina had been the target of Ava's jealousy all day — "they're walking for their boss. Whom they didn't like at first, by the way." Elaine smiled.

"And you?" she added.

"My friend. I mean, she didn't die. And my mother. But that was a long time ago and . . ."

"And what?"

"And it was a long time ago."

"I'm not sure you get your point," Elaine commented gently.

Ava lay in her sleeping bag in the tent, listening to the sound of Elaine's breath moving quietly in and out. She couldn't remember the last time she had shared a sleeping space with a woman older than she was. There had been the aunts in the weeks after her mother died, ready to fold her in their arms at night, but Ava always stayed awake, kicking at carefully designated intervals until another sleeping arrangement was found. She had been like one of those babies in the experiments she read about later in college, given a series of shirts to smell. Only one from the real mother would do. She didn't want impostors.

The truth of it was that since her mother died, she hadn't been good at sleeping with anyone, their breath too close to her face, the way it took over the space so she couldn't sense anything else, couldn't tell what might be coming. Because you never knew.

But Elaine's breathing was soft; the tent was filled with the smell of peppermint and lavender — and chocolate, Ava realized. Elaine had said she was going to steal a brownie from the mess tent for the morning. Ava smiled. The evening had been more fun than she had anticipated, exhausted as she had been when she first reached the tent. But Elaine had insisted she would feel better after a shower — which was true. Ava believed she had never quite enjoyed a shower as much as the one she had in the water truck, surrounded by the usually offensive cacophony of shampoo fragrances of the women around her. But all that mattered was the warmth of the water pouring over her stretched and aching muscles, the feel of the sweat washing out of her hair, the soft fibers of the towel as she ran it over her back and legs. She felt new as her feet relaxed gratefully in a pair of loose-fitting flip-flops.

After dinner, after the last walker had lurched into camp, there had been tryouts for the karaoke contest and Elaine had gotten up and surprised them all with a rousing rendition of "These Boots Were Made for Walking." The applause had pounded against the roof of the capacious dining tent as Elaine bowed, her white hair sweeping the floor. She returned, flushed and laughing, to the table.

"Ava," she said, "you should get up there."

"Not a chance."

"Darling girl," Elaine said, "has anyone ever told you you need to grow down a little?"

Day two, 5:30 in the morning. Ava and Elaine stood in a line waiting for breakfast. Ava said she never had breakfast, but Elaine insisted she eat.

"This is different from regular life," she said. "You need to start filling the tank early in the day."

Elaine was not the only walker with that philosophy and the line at the food tent was long. A group of four women bunched together in front of Elaine and Ava, shivering slightly in the still-dark air; their shirts read "She's My Sister." Ava stood behind them, breathing in the smells of hash browns and onions, fantasizing about hot coffee.

The sisters in front of her had the easy camaraderie of women who had shared bedrooms, forks, crushes on the boy next door. They touched one another without thought, tucking in tags on shirts; their sentences overlapped and finished one another casually, generously, as they talked about their strategies for the day ahead. They were like a perfume, Ava thought, watching them entranced, the top and middle and low notes all playing off one another. The closest she'd ever had to anything like that was with Kate.

One of the sisters commented jokingly about the slowness of the food line and the need for a bathroom, and departed. The group in front of Ava shifted, fragmenting as they watched their sister long after she had disappeared into the accumulating crowd.

"How is she . . . ?"

"Tired."

"But don't . . ."

"I *won't*, God . . ."

The fourth one turned away, looked toward the front of the line.

"Won't it ever move?" she asked.

Their expressions bounced off one another, their hands reaching, touching nothing.

Elaine rested her hand on Ava's shoulder, pulling her attention away from the sisters in front of her. "Will your friend be there at the finish line?" she asked conversationally.

"No; she's on a trip down the Grand Canyon."

"Really?"

And Ava found herself explaining about Kate's victory party and the challenges each of the women had received. "You could tell the rest of them were glad about my getting this," she said, motioning to the scene around her. "They were mad at me; they didn't understand why I wasn't there for her."

"Would you do it that way again?"

"No."

"Well, there you are." They had finally reached the serving line and Elaine took a huge spoonful of potatoes and placed it on Ava's plate. "Oh yes," she said when she saw Ava's reaction, "today's a long one. You'll need every carbohydrate in the county in that skinny little body of yours."

By mile thirty-five, all of Ava's pride in her stamina, her strength, had disappeared. Her hips were wooden clothespins opening and snapping shut with each step. Her focus had narrowed to the pavement in front of her, the pit stops where she could refill her Gatorade bottle and rip open a package of chips or cookies, put moleskin on her blistering toes and heels. She remembered back to her training walks in Los Angeles and her sense of adventure in chasing a smell across the hills behind her house. This was not that. This was not stopping, not getting on one of the vans that followed the course to pick up the walkers who couldn't make it. This was stretching at every stoplight, then feeling the muscles tighten into sharp, tight wires the moment she stepped off the curb. This was walking one foot after the other through the cheering stations where relatives and friends gathered to clap and hug and hand out red licorice and chocolate and tissues. The greeters stood, mothers, fathers, children, friends, holding photographs. Ava was grateful for her dark glasses, the screen they provided.

She looked over at Elaine, who was wearing a picture of her daughter, Diana, safety-pinned to her T-shirt. The woman in the photograph was beautiful — long, black hair, big brown eyes, cheekbones like her mother's. An expression of pure, calm joy. Everyone who walked by commented to Elaine on how stunning her daughter had been. At the pit stops, women came up and hugged her; at the cheering stations, hands would reach out to touch her shoulder as she passed.

"Isn't it hard," Ava asked, "to have them

all talking to you like that?" She remembered when her mother died, how she had taken her mother's favorite perfume bottle and hidden it behind a book on her shelf. She used to pretend that she kept all her memories of her mother in there. She knew what happened to perfume when you opened a bottle.

"You might think so," Elaine said. "But it makes it easier."

Ava looked around her, at the signs and the costumes, the pink feather boas, the sparkled bras worn over T-shirts, the strings of fuchsia-colored beads. It was like being in some strange, huge Mardi Gras parade, with emotion — joy, sadness, exhaustion, determination — worn on the outside along with the lingerie. Trudging along in basic tan, she was at best a backdrop in such a vibrant crowd. But she realized, watching, that it was the people with the photographs who were enveloped in hugs; it was the flamboyant ones who raised the honks from passing cars and the fists held up in the air in salute, providing a moment of distraction and pouring energy over the walkers.

When Ava was young, her mother used to chide her, "You can't just live through your nose, Ava. Get out in the world. Go climb a tree with Kate."

Well, thought Ava, she was out in the world, all right. You can't walk sixty miles with your nose. The image was funny, and Ava smiled. A woman walking past smiled back.

"So tell me something about your mother," Elaine remarked. They had five miles left to go that day and Elaine seemed determined to talk their way through all of them. Already they had covered politics, travel, Ava's past relationships, Elaine's late husband — an eclectic and wide-ranging list of topics that was, Ava had to admit gratefully, diverting. By that point, Ava was feeling almost disembodied, her feet automatically landing one in front of the other, her thoughts wandering. The route was taking them along a jogging trail that followed a slim green river. Every once in a while a runner or biker would pass going in the opposite direction, eyes widening at the flood-tide of pink-garbed women and men. Elaine picked a blackberry off one of the bushes lining the trail and handed it to Ava.

Ava looked down at the fruit in her palm.

"What?" Elaine asked.

"Blackberries," Ava said. "When I was little my parents and I made a pact every April not to eat blackberries until the real

285

ones were ripe in August. Northwest Lent, my dad called it — to make sure you appreciated the real thing."

Ava paused for a moment, then continued, "My mom was the worst at waiting. She used to sneak down to the bushes that grew near the beach, and my dad used to catch her and carry her back to the cottage, both of them laughing. She used to slip blackberry jam onto his toast in revenge, so he would break the pact first, but he always caught her."

Ava put the fruit in her mouth and felt its warmth spread across her tongue, deep and purple, the smell rising up, the essence of summer.

"I always forget how wonderful they taste," she said.

Day three. When Ava woke up, she could sense a change in the air, a rising tide of jubilation in the first murmurings in the tents around her. No matter what, it would be over that day. She checked her watch: 4:15. She declined the option of another half hour of sleep and slipped out of the tent.

At the other end of the camp, she could see the glow of the dining tent where the volunteer crew was already starting to prepare breakfast. Breathing in, she could catch the scent of bacon and hot chocolate, melting butter and scrambled eggs. She felt her stomach growl.

As she returned to her own tent a half hour later, two cups of hot coffee in her hands, Elaine was just putting her head outside, white hair floating about her head.

"Hey there," Ava called out, "ready to finish this sucker off?"

"Good Lord, look who's chipper this morning," said Elaine, as she emerged from the tent and stretched tentatively. She reached over and tucked in the tag on Ava's shirt with a smile, then took the coffee and let the steam rise up into her face.

There was something about knowing they were heading for a finish line that made the walking easier. Miles slid past, generosity bloomed. At pit stops, strangers applied moleskin to each other's feet and laughed at jokes that would have gotten failing grades in any other situation. Conversations moved along the line of walkers, bouncing off the pavement only to be caught by others and passed forward or backward. Ava could still feel every step she took, a sharp vibration that hummed up her shins and pulled tight in the back of her legs, but she could imagine the end and the pain no longer mattered.

She thought of her mother and Kate, of what it must have been like, what it must be like, never knowing if or when it would be over, or what over would look like when you got there. The thought turned her spine cold and she was grateful for the certain knowledge of miles remaining to the finish, of the celebration waiting when she got there.

Around two in the afternoon, the volunteers at the pit stops started calling out the miles: "Five to go!" "Two-point-seven!" Teams started chanting, taking old army drills and modifying them while their feet stomped along the pavement. The pace accelerated. Ava could hear the lungs around her filling and exhaling faster and deeper; she could smell the fragrances of Bengay and perfume and deodorant thicken and grow with the rising heat of the walkers. As they got down to the last half mile, they encountered what looked like a continuous cheering station, the sound of applause rolling toward them, buffeting Ava.

Behind her dark glasses, Ava felt tears falling down her cheeks. She looked quickly over at Elaine, who was crying.

"It's okay," Elaine said to Ava. "It's okay."

Then they turned the corner and entered

the home stretch, lined with people three and four deep holding up hand-painted signs, pumping fists in the air, one woman standing silently, as if holding in a sound that would deafen the rest of the crowd.

The closing ceremonies were over and family members were starting to find one another. An impossibly tall man with white beginning to fleck into his hair came out of the crowd and hugged Elaine long and hard.

"I am so proud of you," he said. "Look at what you did."

"Ava, this is my son Adam," Elaine explained as she stepped back, smiling.

The man put out his hand; Ava moved forward to take it, leaning in. Kate always joked that Ava was like a dog, smelling every man, woman and child to sense if they were friend or foe.

"Nice to meet you," Adam said, bending toward her, covering her hand in his. Ava inhaled, caught something, but it was immediately lost in the hailstorm of smells around them.

"I'm Ava," she replied. Just then she heard her name yelled at top volume. Across the crowd she saw her father and Sara and Hadley, Sara's twins on the women's shoulders, big and little hands flying in the air.

"I have to go," she said. She turned to Elaine and hugged her for a long moment. "I have your number; I'll call."

It wasn't until she was across the crowd, after Sara and Hadley and her father had swept her up in a hug that lifted her off her feet, that her mind placed the scent. Blackberries.

KATE

No one had told her the part about peeing, Kate thought as she held on to the side of the huge yellow raft, her body half-submerged in water that seemed to freeze in place even as it moved past her. She watched the girls in the river around her — and they were still girls, Kate thought, no matter that they called themselves women — casually hanging on to the side of the boat as if they were ordering margaritas at the local bar, their conversations dancing in the air even as their bladders released into the river about them. Then with a laugh, they vaulted effortlessly up into the raft.

Kate gripped the rope that ran along the side of the boat, tightened her sphincter muscles to no effect, and hated the girls, even as she remained proudly awestruck at the slim elegance of her daughter, who now looked down at her from the safety of the raft, her face shadowed with concern.

"How're you doing, Mom?" Robin asked.

Kate gritted her teeth. Or maybe they were chattering. The water really was cold, after all. How could river water be so cold when the air had reached well over one hundred degrees? Hot. Cold. Three hours into the trip, and so far subtle was not a word she would use to describe the Grand Canyon.

"Oh, fine."

"Seriously, Mom."

Patty the river guide, the ten-foot-long oars of the raft resting easily in her hands, looked over her shoulder at Kate.

"If the water's too cold, you can get back in the raft and just pee over the side."

It took Kate a moment to understand. This woman sitting above her, with her long muscled arms and terra-cotta tan, was suggesting that Kate hang her naked white buttocks off the side of the raft and pee into the air. There were five other boats. Kate had a sudden, full-color memory of walking down hospital corridors, one hand holding the IV stand, the other behind her, gripping her gown together in back.

"I thought I was done with flashing my ass," Kate said in an undertone to her daughter.

"I'd turn the boat around," Patty added

helpfully. "Upriver."

Actually, the rest of their rafts were well ahead of them by now, but there were other groups on the river, motorized expeditions, their rafts huge moving-van affairs that came flying down the river, their approach announced by the roar of their engines only moments before their arrival.

"I can wait until we stop," Kate said. She figured her bladder was probably frozen by now, anyway.

It took three of the healthy young girls, joking companionably, to pull Kate back into the raft, two grabbing her arms, Robin finishing off the project by hauling Kate in by the waistband of her shorts. Kate landed on her belly in the raft, rolled over and sprawled against the side, breathing, and felt her bladder begin to defrost.

Camp that evening was on a sandbar stretching warm and soft along the edge of the river, framed by stands of tamarisk trees, their branches leggy and graceful, silvery leaves shifting in the breeze. Once the gear had been unloaded, dry bags tossed fireman-style in a chain from boat to beach, their group had spread out, the veteran rafters setting up their tents, eager to claim the shady and protected spots, while others lounged by the river with books in hand. At the far end of the beach Kate saw Robin, washing her hair with the group of younger women, jumping back from the cold water, shaking their heads so the drops flew away from them in sunlit arcs.

Two of the guides were setting up the kitchen, digging in ammo boxes and the huge metal coolers for the utensils and ingredients for the evening's meal. Kate walked up to the head guide, Sam, who stood at a makeshift table chopping onions.

"Can I help?" she asked. Sam appeared close to her age and was wearing a wedding band — two facts she found curious as she had always thought of river guides as young, with wild hair and wilder sex lives — but which also made approaching him easier.

"We're probably fine, if you want to read or relax," Sam said easily. It amazed Kate how calm the guides were, how casually they seemed to navigate waves or rumpled emotions. She herself felt like one of the dry bags, tossed from one experienced hand to another, capable of exactly nothing.

Let me do something I know how to do, she silently begged.

Sam looked over at her thoughtfully.

"Well, you could chop the green peppers." He handed her the knife and took another one out of the case.

The knife felt good in her hand, simple and straightforward. She stood the pepper on its end and sliced down, feeling the quick crunch of the outer skin, the way the knife fell through the hollow space inside, the solid thump as the knife connected with the cutting board below. The brisk, spicy smell jumped up to meet her nose as she cleaned out the seeds and the stiff white flesh. Her fingers instinctively moved out of the way of the sharp edge of the knife as she cut quick, regular slices, and she found herself breathing easily for the first time that day. She looked up at the cliffs across from her, the late afternoon light playing among the layers, the air turning pink and ever-lightening shades of blue between the canyon walls. The water ran green in front of her, clear and cold.

"It's gorgeous here," she said quietly. "It feels as if the whole world is gone." She laughed. "I bet everybody says that."

"You know," Sam commented, "in a couple days you won't be able to even see the top of the canyon anymore."

"How's that?"

"The river goes down." He said it without a trace of condescension, as if not realizing that a river had to go downhill was the most logical thing in the world. "We'll go through two hundred million years of rock, and even the top layer is as old as the dinosaurs. Pretty amazing. Each layer has its own colors and textures. Kaibab, Toroweap, Coconino, Hermit, Supai, Redwall, Muav, Bright Angel, Tapeats." He made it sound like the names of children he knew and loved, although Kate couldn't imagine how many times he must have rattled off the list. "My favorite is Redwall." He saw her face. "Want to know how to remember them all?"

She nodded.

"Know The Canyon's History; Study Rocks Made By Time."

"Or," Patty said wickedly as she passed by, a metal box and a toilet seat in her hands, "Kissing Takes Concentration, However Some Require More Breath and Tongue. Thanks for the groover duty, by the way, Sam, my man." And she was off, down the beach.

"Get a view of the river, Patty!" Sam called after her cheerfully.

"Groover duty?"

"You'll see," Sam said with a wink. "Better not to explain while cooking."

"Today we are going to see our first rapid." Sam stood with his back to the rumbling green river, addressing the group, who sat cross-legged on the sand, gripping their mugs of coffee with the territorial protectiveness of people who are not used to getting out of sleeping bags at 5:30 in the morning. "Not huge, by any means — we don't get those until the second half of the trip — but it'll be good practice. Who wants to go in the paddle boat?"

The girls' hands shot up, Robin's among them. Robin looked at her mother sitting next to her and lowered her arm.

"I want to do today with you," she said.

"You're not the mother, Robin."

"Exactly my point." Robin grinned.

On an ordinary day, on the flat peaceful canvas of a lake, the paddle boat would have appeared substantial — a friendly yellow bus with room for six paddlers, lined up three on each side, and a guide at the back. Set in the context of the wide green river in front of them, compared with the eighteen-foot-long oar boats with their mountains of gear, the paddle boat shrank, a rubber duck among freighter ships. Kate watched the girls excitedly donning their waterproof pants and jackets, saw how Sam moved among them, carefully cinching up the side straps of their life jackets.

"You want it secure," he replied matter-of-factly when one of the girls squealed.

Kate felt her stomach clench. She couldn't remember where the fear had come from — a movie, a story, a dream, the one where the person is trapped below a boat or a layer of thick blue ice, underwater in any case, unable to find the surface. A memory of a moment that had not yet occurred, that last, long minute before her lungs surrendered to water, praying for gills that didn't exist.

It was almost funny how much it scared her. You would think, having looked in the mirror and seen the lines of her skull beneath her skin, she would be immune from concerns about mortality. The get-out-of-death-free card, as Robin called it. But life had an odd sense of humor, it appeared, becoming more precious rather than less, each particular moment made more beautiful with the sense that it had been paid for, earned. Or perhaps it was simply that after skirting the precipitous edge of extinction, it would be too ironic to drown.

She looked at the big, muscular water and tightened the side straps of her life jacket.

"Do you want to go with Patty again?" Robin was asking. Kate considered the question. She felt a need for a masculine size and strength at the oars for this rapid, but she had already floated with Patty, trusted her. Maybe there would be a karmic advantage for putting your feminist ideals to the test. Kate liked that idea.

"Sure," she said, grabbing her water bottles.

She and Robin were the only two in the big oar boat along with Patty, who sat above them on the rectangular metal cooler that spanned the width of the boat, one long, wooden oar held casually in each hand.

"Today's a piece of cake, girls," she said, eyes alight under her cowboy hat, ropy arms relaxed at her sides. "Just enough clouds to keep us cool; not enough for rain. Some good water, but not too big. You'll do great."

Kate and Robin perched on the sides of the raft at the front.

"When we get near the rapid," Patty remarked, "you're going to brace one foot against the side of the raft and hold on to a rope with each hand. No letting go." Patty looked pointedly at Kate, and Robin laughed. The day before, when they had reached one of the larger riffles, Kate had instinctively put out her hand to hold Robin in the raft. "Soccer mom arm," Patty had called it.

"Mom, if you fly out of the boat trying to keep me in it, I'm going to be really mad at you," Robin said with a smile as they settled into their positions.

"I get it," Patty commented to Kate from her position on the cooler. "I've got a kid at home."

Kate looked up at her, shocked. "You do?"

"Eight years old. Little guy is smart as a whip."

Patty pushed the oar boat off from the bank and joined the rest of the flotilla bobbing downriver like a lazy herd of cows. She sat at ease, dipping the oars into the water and propelling the boat forward just enough to steer, letting the river do the rest of the work. Kate felt the motion of the water as she gazed at the canyon walls that rose far above her. Already they were deeper in the canyon, carried by a river that had been running for six million years, each curve in the riverbed, each mile taking them somewhere older, more primitive.

What would it be like, Kate wondered, to leave your eight-year-old child at home and go throw yourself into the rapids? Even when Robin was a small child, Robin had always been more comfortable leaving Kate than Kate had been leaving her. It wasn't just the prospect of losing Robin — although the thought of that sliced through Kate like a hot wire — since the time Robin was born, Kate had become aware of her own vulnerability in a new and different way. She buckled her seat belt, even on a half-mile trip to the grocery store, because she couldn't stand the thought of her daughter growing up wondering why her mother hadn't loved her enough to be careful. She stopped skiing black diamond routes, bought a Volvo, pulling in the world of her activities to a circle that would always remain safe, the same. Rick had commented about her becoming domesticated, but Kate, looking at the wonder of her sleeping little girl, sprawled across her crib like a claim-jumper, knew that wasn't it. Hers was a deal made with fate — I will give up these parts of my life if you will keep my girl safe, keep me safe for her. It was only at the meeting with the oncologist almost three years ago that she had learned that there were no deals, only options.

"Okay," Patty declared, joy in her voice, "here we go!" Kate closed her eyes and they flew down into a blast of liquid green ice. Before Kate could even scream, they were out the other side.

The mood was excited that night; it seemed everyone was full of tales of their adventures on the water. The paddle boat girls radiated the satisfied glow of honeymooners, stretching their newly found confidence and touching one another with ease. The veteran rafters — and to Kate's eyes, this meant just about everyone but her — looked at the girls indulgently and swapped stories of past trips while they filtered river water for drinking.

Kate didn't know where she fit into this group. The past three years had made her feel as old as the river they traveled down, but faced with her minimal rafting experience, she felt younger than the girls. She didn't know what to do with all the sky; she didn't know who she was without a roof over her head. She wanted to be brave and strong for her daughter, but she didn't know what those words meant here where everything was heat and sand and water.

She climbed over an outcropping of rock and saw a small curve in the river, just large enough to slow the current into a private eddy. The two older women in their group, Madge and Rita, were by the water. Madge was washing Rita's hair and they were laughing. Kate started to retreat, but they spotted her and waved her down to them.

"It feels so much better to have someone wash your hair," Madge called out. "Want to join us?"

At the initial introductions at the put-in spot at Lee's Ferry, Kate had learned that

Madge and Rita were in their mid-sixties, friends who had been rafting the Grand Canyon together since they were in their twenties. Every year they left behind husbands and families to travel down the rapids. Robin had found them fascinating, and she and Kate had spent the first day in their raft speculating on the lives these women had when they weren't on the river. Robin opted for the superhero story line, summoning a vision of women who wore aprons and baked cookies and then went into a gas station restroom near Lee's Ferry and emerged in quick-dry pants and orange life vests. Kate had hoped for broken glass ceilings at home as well as on the river.

In the end, as they had found out over dinner that night, the reality was somewhere in the middle, which was only to be expected. Rita was a hospital nurse, a wife and mother of four grown children. Madge worked with homeless youth, had a son who was a lawyer, another whose occupation seemed vague.

But here, on the river, they were two women washing each other's hair, and the softness of it melted Kate's hesitation and she wove her way through the rocks toward them.

"I always forget how cold the river is," Rita

said to Kate, gasping as Madge poured a bucket of water over her lowered head.

"And then" — she wrung out her long, white hair like a rope and flung it up and over so it landed with a smack against her back — "I remember how good it feels to be clean."

"So, Kate, is this your first time on the river?" Madge asked.

Kate nodded, thinking how nice it was that some people could make a question whose answer was so stunningly obvious still sound like an honest inquiry.

"What do you think?"

"I feel like an idiot." The words jumped out of Kate's mouth, unbidden.

"Lean over," Madge directed Kate, pointing to the water. Kate felt the shock of the water pouring over her head and the comforting pressure of strong fingers working their way into her hair, her scalp. She remembered Robin, washing her hair over the sink when she felt too queasy to stand in the shower, remembered sitting on the couch, painting each other's toenails bright blue because, Robin had insisted, Kate needed to have something fun to look at when she was in the hospital. The feeling of her daughter's hands, holding her foot, warm and gentle.

She was not going to cry.

Madge's fingers kept moving, firmly and rhythmically.

"Well then, we like you," she said.

And Kate told them everything.

The group of hikers sloshed along the stream and scrambled up serpentine cliffs, conversations moving among them, stories becoming a psychological shelter against the heat. The rock walls of the side canyon reflected the hot afternoon sun; the few tamarisk saplings they passed sent off a dry, sepia-toned scent. For Kate, who was accustomed to walking trails through the evergreens of the Pacific Northwest on days that were rarely hot even in July, it had felt strange at first to be in a terrain and climate where hiking more often meant rock climbing or wading and the sun had a power that demanded obedience.

But she was reaching a plateau of comfort here on the river, she realized. She still couldn't jump in and out of a boat with anything approaching grace, but after only a few nights she had come to love the firm feel of sand under her sleeping bag. Her reading glasses were lost somewhere in the depths of her dry bag, and now she spent most of her evenings contemplating the cliffs and the sky. And she no longer thought twice about hiking through water or sweating through her shirt. It would all be dry or wet again in moments, anyway, she thought as she looked at the trail up ahead, so it really didn't matter.

They heard the waterfall before they saw it, a tumbling of water, but sweeter, gentler than a rapid. They rounded the corner and the creek turned into a deeper pool, backed by a series of fern- and moss-covered rocks and ledges, water pouring down over it all, spilling in silken threads into the pool.

"Elves live here," Robin said in a voice Kate hadn't heard since her daughter was young.

The young men in the group instantly threw themselves into the water and swam across the pool, climbing up a hidden route behind the rocks, emerging onto the upper ledges and leaping off with a whoop into the water. Robin and the other girls soon followed. Kate stood back, watching as they landed in the pool and then sprang to the surface, breasts jostling within the confines of their sports bras and bikini tops. Some things you couldn't fake with prosthetic bras, she thought.

Kate had insisted on a double mastectomy,

although it hadn't been mandatory. By that point, her breasts were alien to her, a body part that had fed a baby and now grew death. She wanted it gone. Them gone, if that's what it meant. And for most of the time, it was possible to believe that not having breasts didn't matter. Undressing only happened twice a day and she had gotten rid of the full-length mirror when Rick had moved out years before, taking her sex life with him as if it had been packed in a box along with his sports equipment. It had taken years for her to even think about dating, and just when she was ready there was the diagnosis and her calendar was suddenly full with a new form of rendezvous, bar drinks replaced with other liquids that altered her state of mind.

Caroline and Marion had talked to Kate about reconstructive surgery but she always deflected the conversation, joking that there had never been much to reconstruct, anyway. Which meant she didn't have to say that she already felt less than real, her body more chemicals than flesh, her life borrowed. She didn't need to borrow any more.

She wished she could be like the woman in the photograph Marion had given her after the surgery. A woman with arms outspread, face to the sky in celebration, one breast full and firm, the other simply not there. Kate had put the photograph in the back of her closet.

Sam came up next to her with the last of their group. One guide was always the sweeper, bringing along the stragglers.

"Are you going in?" he said. "You'll be amazed how good clean water feels."

"Maybe just to get wet." Kate waded in, waist deep. She watched her daughter emerge from behind the first ledge, standing in an alcove of dripping green moss as if about to recite a monologue from *A Midsummer Night's Dream.* Robin waved to her mother and jumped, her excited yelp cut off by her entry into the water. The water was cool, not cold, and miraculously sweet-smelling.

Sam walked over to Madge and Rita and talked with them, their voices happy and quiet. Kate thought she saw Madge motioning toward Kate, but she might well have been simply pointing out the antics of Troy, the young buck guide playing in the water behind her. After ten minutes or so, Sam did his summoning whistle.

"Okay, guys," he yelled. "Out you get. Gals-only pool for a while."

"What?" the men in the group protested.

"Really?"

"It's tradition," Sam said calmly. "We go back and start dinner. Gals do the dishes later."

As Sam left at the back of the pack of men, he passed Patty. Kate heard her say in a low voice, "Since when, Sam?"

With the men gone, the pool quieted. The girls swam lazily, congregating in a small group under the flow of the waterfall, pressure-washing their hair. Patty had climbed up several ledges and sat with her eyes closed, her face peaceful and private. The other women relaxed along the rocks or floated on their backs, looking up at the sky. Madge and Rita lounged on a ledge, swinging their feet in the water like children.

"Okay," Madge called out, "the guys are gone, we can skinny-dip!"

The girls under the waterfall looked over in surprise.

"We do it every year," said Madge. "But usually, we're just sneaking in a quick dip upriver from camp."

At the top of the waterfall, Patty stood up, grinning, and pulled her sports bra over her head, tossing it into the pool below. The girls under the waterfall laughed and started taking off bathing suits and shorts.

Rita unbuttoned the long-sleeved sun protection shirt she always wore and casually dropped it on the rock ledge, followed by her tank top and shorts. She stood on the rock, naked and at ease, her legs long, her stomach soft, her breasts heavy and relaxed.

"Your hat," Madge prompted her, and Rita laughed, taking off her baseball cap and letting her white hair fall loose about her shoulders.

She was beautiful, Kate thought.

Rita lowered herself in the water, smiling at the contact of the water against her skin. She looked over at Kate.

"Now you," Rita said. "And yes, you are."

"What?"

"Beautiful."

Kate turned her back on the group and unbuttoned her shirt, feeling the sun against her stomach, her chest. She undid the hooks on her bathing suit, the prosthetic padding heavy in her hands, like small, dead bags of rice, and laid it on the rocks next to her. In the sun, the scars were still purple-red, cutting across her. Tire tracks, she always called them, from the truck that ran her over.

She sank down into the water and the coolness welcomed her, running along her skin, the reflected light playing over the scars like soft fingers. She looked at the green of the moss and ferns, at the rocks around her, rounded by air and water, heaved and fallen into place, making a pool for the water to spill into. Quiet. There.

"So I've got a question for you." Kate and Robin were setting up their tent for the night, shaking out the nylon fabric between them and laying it flat on the ground.

"What's that?" Robin asked.

"Why this trip?"

"You mean, why not a spa?" Robin's voice shimmered with amusement.

"Well, yes."

"I don't know." Robin paused. She threaded a long metal pole through the loops on the outside of the tent and then found a rock to place on the corner. "I guess — after the last couple years — I just wanted to be scared by something I could put my hands on. Does that make sense?"

Kate nodded.

"I should've really asked you, though."

"No." Kate laughed quietly. "I would have said no."

Robin grinned. "That's what I figured."

The guides had warned them about rattle-snakes, had directed them not to lay out their sleeping bags ahead of time and to carry a flashlight if they were going to the groover in the dark. Kate had seen the evidence — undulating trails left in the sand and disappearing between rocks. Initially she had been terrified at the prospect of the hollow clatter of rattles, the spiraling muscle of a snake body, but that fear had dissipated as the days passed.

So it was a shock to see the rattlesnake coiled across the path, lazy in the late afternoon sun. She stopped, suddenly aware of how hopelessly cumbersome her feet were, slapping about in her flip-flops, how exposed her legs were in her nylon shorts, a target expansive as a Kansas cornfield. But the rattlesnake moved not at all, as if any interest in her was easily outweighed by the satisfaction of warm sand and hot sun.

She stood, caught in indecision. She wondered if she was more likely to spook the rattlesnake if she moved later rather than sooner, but in the end, she was unable even to shift her weight in preparation to leave.

"Good job." She heard Madge's voice behind her. "Just relax."

And as Madge spoke, the rattlesnake uncurled itself and moved farther down the trail to where, Kate saw with a start, another rattlesnake, smaller and lighter in color, emerged from the bushes. The two snakes circled each other.

"Hold still," Madge said, her voice reverent.

"What?"

"Wait; you'll see."

The snakes moved toward each other, bodies sliding over and under, rising up, extravagantly high, a flowing contrast of white bellies and dark backs, climbing each other in a constantly moving helix, their heads weaving apart, then together. At some point, gravity and balance would pull them back to the ground, where they would start again. As Kate watched their movements, unending, sinuous, she felt a tug in her belly, a feeling of slowly moving gears.

"Incredible," she said in a hushed voice.

"The river must want you to be here," Madge said, "to show you that."

Somewhere around the sixth day, time had discarded standard forms of measurement. It hung effortlessly in the air at night, stretched as they waited at the top of a rapid, snapping tight like a rubber band as they shot through the heaving water. It expanded huge and golden as they hiked up slot canyons, cooked dinner, played Frisbee in a giant arching cavern that could easily have sheltered twenty groups their size. As paddlers on the river, they got up while it was barely light, went to bed with the sun without ever checking watches, which few of them still wore, anyway.

At the confluence of the Little Colorado River, the big river had changed from green to brown, becoming thick and gritty, an amphibious creature, half dirt, half water, so solid at times Kate almost thought it might walk up out of its banks. At night the sky was filled with so many stars it seemed as if the darkness was peeking through a wash of light. In this world, hair was something you wet down to keep you cool, fingernails were tools, not adornment.

When they reached Phantom Ranch, a halfway point where some trips picked up and dropped off passengers who either hiked in or out the ten-mile trail to the top of the rim, they were startled by even the rustic signs of habitation there, at the sharp edges of civilization still clinging to those who had hiked in that morning. That night at camp, the guides told them that they were about to enter the gorge, where the walls narrowed even further.

"Okay," declared Sam, "we're coming to a big one now." He steered the paddle boat into an eddy where it bobbed, out of the current, restless but stationary. Kate listened; she could hear the rapid up ahead, growling and crashing, a level of noise unlike any she had heard before in the trip, and her stomach wrapped around itself and tightened up toward her lungs, making her breath short and shallow.

She remembered the doctor at the hospital, the one whose brown eyes were kind above his mask, asking her, "Kate, are you remembering to breathe these days?" As if you could forget. Except of course you did, perhaps even on purpose, as if in the back of your mind you suspected that you had only been allotted so many breaths in your life, a number designated on the day you were born, precious inhalations and exhalations that you had given up so unthinkingly throughout your life, walking to the post office, kissing a boy you should never have dated in the first place. Breath you held on to now because each one out felt like one less left.

"Breath is life in, Kate," the doctor had said, as if he knew. "Not life out."

Sitting in the eddy, feeling the river licking the sides of the paddle boat, Kate took a deep inhalation, swelling her lungs, feeling the air flow into her arms, her stomach, pushing down against the tightness. Her hands gripped the paddle and she looked back at Sam.

"Now, Hermit has lots of ups and downs," Sam was explaining, "but it's a fun one. Just do what I tell you when I tell you and don't forget to brace a foot against the side of the boat; it'll help hold you in. We won't tip over, but if we do there are oar boats ahead and behind us to pick you up.

"Lead paddlers" — Sam nodded at Kate and Arnie — "you're setting the pace. The other paddlers go only as fast as you do, so when I say, you two dig with those paddles as if there's treasure in China, okay?" He smiled the Sam smile, the one that would make even the businesswoman who still steadfastly applied mascara every morning pack up her own tent and carry it down to the boats.

Kate nodded. How had she ended up in the paddle boat, in this seat, today? She honestly couldn't remember. It had been such a blur, getting on the life jackets, Sam cinching them tight. They'd been joking about Mammy and Scarlett and corsets, and he handed her a paddle and she stepped into the only place left in the boat, too nervous to notice the significance of her position. Rule of life, Kate noted with irony, always know your seat in the boat before you set out.

"Everybody ready?" Sam asked, and Kate realized there was no option to say no. With rock walls rising high above their heads and a river flowing at a rate of tens of thousands of cubic feet per second, there was only one way you could go, and only one way to do it — after Phantom Ranch, hiking out was no longer a possibility, the only exit by emergency helicopter or the take-out point a week downriver. For Kate, after living in the cancer world where it seemed there was always another experimental medicine, another course of treatment, where the promise of success was carefully protected behind an ever-changing wall of percentages and statistics, the reality of the river was stark.

"Let's get in line then," Sam said. "Easy paddling for now."

Kate saw the rapid before the other paddlers, its angry brown water pitching and roiling, white spray exploding up in all directions. Kate watched as Patty's oar boat met and crashed through the first wave, disappearing under the river and shuddering up like a horse pulling itself out of the thick mud-water. Thousands of pounds of water. Kate had never thought of water as weight before, but she did now, as she watched it churning upon itself, clawing at the sides of the canyon it had created.

This water eats rocks, Kate thought, in a moment of clarity. I am in a rubber boat.

"Our turn," Sam directed, and the paddle boat moved steadily forward, and then down the smooth tongue of water into the rapid. Kate looked at the first wave coming at her, their speed suddenly fast, saw its arc, how it would rise, was rising, above her head, and she reached down and stuck her paddle in the river. The boat moved forward, but not enough; they wouldn't quite clear the crest. The top of it blasted over her, drenching her arms and face.

She shook her head to clear the water from her eyes. When she opened them she saw another wave. Her arms flailed, running the paddle across the top of the water that moved toward her, the wave too close, too fast.

"Paddle hard!" Sam yelled from the back of the boat.

She took a quick look at Arnie, who was paddling rapidly, steadily next to her. She aimed her paddle at the water, trying to keep pace with him. The wave smashed into them, sideswiping her with a wall of freezing water. Their boat wasn't flipping, but she knew she was doing nothing to help them stay upright.

Panicked, she shoved her foot farther into the gap between the rim of the boat and the base and felt it catch in one of the straps for her water bottle. She yanked at her foot; it didn't move. She'd never get out if they tipped, she realized with a flash of shock.

"Dig!" Sam yelled. Kate looked up and saw the next wave, higher than the last, and fear poured through her. Her foot was a block of weight, trapped in the straps. She saw the water rearing up to claim her boat, suck it under the wave, ready to throw her out and chew her up against the rocks. She raised her paddle high and felt pain spark across the scars on her chest.

"You son of a *bitch,*" she spat out, the water snatching the words from her mouth even as she said them.

She hefted higher, reaching above her shoulders for height and force, and plunged the blade in, pulling it toward her against the resistance of the cold, greedy water. Again, higher, harder, up, down, in, pull, feeling every muscle, shoulders and arms reaching up, slamming down — fear and hate and anger coursing through and out of her body until she thought that the rage of the water must be made from her.

"That's it!" Sam yelled as they vaulted over the top. The next wave roared into view in front of them, huge. *"Dig now!"*

She could sense Arnie next to her, matching her pace, upping it. She could feel the other paddlers behind her, all of them together pushing their ridiculous seedpod of a boat through this hurricane of a river. Seeing the next wave rising, impossibly, twenty feet tall, she launched her weight forward, almost out of the boat, letting her tangled foot anchor her, raising her paddle high up into the wave coming at her, digging in, again and again, climbing the wall of water like a ladder, feeling the paddlers straining behind her, taking the boat up, up, up until they were past the crest and plummeting down the other side.

They rocketed their way over the next three waves, each of them easier, until suddenly it was over and they coasted into a current that traveled quietly downstream, a few ripples on its surface, like the hiccups of a child at the end of a tantrum.

"Yes!" Sam cheered, and their team held paddles in the air over their heads in a victory salute. Kate reached up, breathing hard, feeling the strength of her arms, the power of her legs and lungs.

"You were great," Arnie said to Kate, his

eyes sweeping over her appreciatively. Kate smiled and bent over to work at the strap around her foot. Arnie watched her, curious, and then saw what she was doing.

"Oh, man . . ." he said, and shook his head, eyes large.

"Well, at least it would've been easy to find the body," Kate remarked. She and Arnie looked at each other and started laughing, big, huge gasps filled with air and no easier to control.

Robin's oar boat pulled up next to them and started bailing water. Kate thought what a lumbering beast it seemed next to their sweet, trustworthy little paddle boat. How beautiful her daughter looked, her hair and life jacket dripping water, her eyes alight.

"Wow, Mom," Robin called over, "you were something else out there."

Kate shot Arnie a warning look; he returned it with a gaze of innocence. "Didn't know she had it in her, did you?" he called back to Robin.

Kate slipped out of her sleeping bag and slid down to the bottom of the tent, unzipping the flaps quietly so as not to wake Robin. It was still warm outside and the moon was almost full, illuminating the sand

and scrub brush around her. She had to pee, of course. She could walk to the groover — a name whose origin she still didn't understand — or she could go relieve herself at the water's edge. The latter was closer, and there was less chance of stepping on a sleeping rattlesnake on the trail. Kate slipped her feet into her flip-flops and made her way cautiously to the shore.

She crouched with her toes at the edge of the water, feeling the air move across her exposed skin. She could hear the rapids upriver, and the ones that waited for her tomorrow. But here in an eddy the water lapped with friendly insistence against the sand. Kate relaxed, feeling the liquid leaving her body and entering the river, then looked up to see a sky overwhelmed with stars, their light covering the vast darkness like sugar spilled across a counter.

"Oh my God," she whispered. She pulled up her shorts and sat back on the sand, staring up, breathing in the river air, the sound of the rapids moving through her body. Her shoulders, which she thought would be aching after the exertion of the day, relaxed.

And then, like an unexpected punch in the stomach, she was crying. Sobbing, her hand covering her mouth in a desperate attempt to muffle the sound, her breath heaving in and out of her lungs as if she was going under for the third time. She rocked forward, head reaching toward her crossed legs, then back. She couldn't stop. The river was loud, but she felt the need to get away so no one would hear.

She stood up, still gasping, and walked upriver away from the tents, her vision blurred. She reached a spot where a huge rock, twice her height, rose out of the water and she huddled beside it, her body beaten by sobs that wouldn't stop, even as a part of her mind, the rational part, looked for a reason and found none. Still she sobbed, and for the first time in her life she was unable to control it. All those months of chemo, chemicals ripping through her body, hundreds of hours crunched over a toilet, shaking in bed, feeling people prick and scan and cut her body, sweeping up her hair, her life, from the floor, and she had always been able to stop crying, but not now. She gave up and leaned into the sobs, feeling them wash over her, pulling up breath from the bottom of her stomach.

She wasn't sure how long it was until the sobs finally slowed. She washed her face in the river water, hands shaking, and watched its dark surface moving in front of her like a great secret. After a while, she realized she was cold, and she stood.

"You okay?"

The words came out of the night behind her. Kate recognized Sam's voice.

"Oh, hell," she said under her breath. She turned around, hands gripping her upper arms. She could just make out Sam's form under a sleeping bag laid out about twenty feet above the river line. "I thought the guides were sleeping at the other end."

"I like the privacy." His voice held a smiling irony. He sat up. "Don't worry; you aren't the first person who's cried to the river. Are you cold?"

She nodded, and made a movement to return downstream.

"Maybe you should give yourself a few minutes before you go back," Sam said. "I don't think you're ready yet."

"How do you know?"

"Like I said." He stood up, turned his inflatable pad parallel to the river and sat back down on one end of it.

"Want a seat?" he asked.

She walked up closer, looking at his face in the moonlight.

"Not to worry," he said, pointing to the band on his ring finger.

She dropped down on the pad and he took the opened sleeping bag and draped it across their shoulders. They sat next to each other, looking out to the dark water in front of them.

"I don't know what that was," she said, embarrassment lingering in her words.

"They say the canyon holds everything that everyone has let out here," Sam remarked. "It just hits some people more than others." He was quiet for a while, the heat of their bodies warming the space under the sleeping bag.

"Madge told me," he said, still looking at the water.

"I figured."

"How're you doing?"

"Cleared for takeoff, as Robin would say. Landing uncertain."

"You've got a good daughter," Sam commented. "I see how she watches you."

"I got lucky with her." Kate smiled a bit to herself.

"Where is her father?"

Kate listened for suggestion or judgment in his voice, and sensed none. "We got divorced when Robin was in middle school."

She heard the intake of Sam's breath. "It must've been rough, being on your own for all this," he said quietly.

"I've got incredible friends," Kate said. "It's Robin I worry about."

"She'll be fine, you know."

Kate pulled her knees toward her and felt the smooth surface of a rock under her right foot. She leaned forward and picked it up, feeling its weight in her hand, the cool air outside. She pulled her hand back into the warmth of the opened sleeping bag. How long had it been, Kate wondered, since she had sat next to a man like this, felt the heat coming off his arms and legs, mingling with her own? The simple, intimate comfort of sharing space.

"It's funny," she said after a while, her voice contemplative, "when Robin was little, she was so independent — she didn't need anyone taking care of her, but it was all I wanted to do. I didn't know how not to." Kate shook her head. "It's what broke up my marriage."

"How so?"

"My husband said he didn't want to be married to Robin's mother anymore."

"Oh."

"Yeah." Kate took a breath. "So, what do you do when you're not here?"

"I teach English."

"Really?" Kate looked over at him, surprised.

"Yeah. I was a river rat when I was younger. I gave it up for a while there when

I got married — I had this idea of what grown-ups were supposed to be like — but I missed the river. Now I come every August and do a couple trips."

"What does your wife think about that?"

"She was the one who called my old boss and told him I needed to come back." Sam laughed.

Kate tried to imagine picking up a phone, making the call. "So, how many times have you been down the river?" she asked.

"About a hundred."

"That's why you can get us through a rapid like that."

"You did pretty well yourself today."

Kate shook her head. "I don't know where that came from, either."

"You will." She could hear his smile in the dark.

Kate walked back along the river, feeling the air riffling quietly along her skin. She felt shaken, hollow, but somehow completely, perfectly clean. She couldn't remember the last time that had been true.

She wasn't the first one to cry to the river, Sam had said. She looked out at the big water, thinking about all the anger and sadness and love it must hold. People would tell things to a river they wouldn't tell their friends. At least the ones they thought were going to live.

She had been a river, she thought as she walked back along its bank, the one they all told things to. Caroline, Daria, Marion, Sara, Hadley, Ava — it seemed that when they were around someone who might or might not be there the next year, they said things they wouldn't otherwise, let out parts of themselves they might normally keep hidden. Kate wondered sometimes now if they remembered what they had said and who they had been during those times.

Daria, always so spiky, so angry. Bringing her that odd bread on the red plate. Taking Kate into her studio where she never let anyone go, sitting Kate at her wheel with the clay, starting the movement of the wheel and then leaving. Kate's hands on the clay, like touching silence, all the voices of the doctors and nurses gone, the clay beneath her fingers molding to her touch, the lightest impression of her finger creating a ridge, the upward movement making the clay rise between her hands.

Hadley, showing her the big blue chair in her overgrown garden and telling Kate it was for her, whenever she needed a place to be by herself. Kate sitting in the chair in the sun, hearing Hadley playing next door with

Sara's twins, the longing in Hadley's voice clear and strong. Sara, coming over to Hadley's garden and sitting on the ground next to Kate, her hands playing with the vines as if she could find herself within the tangle of ivy.

Marion in the hospital waiting room with Kate, making up stories about the people who surrounded them, turning ordinary strangers into retired circus performers and safecrackers, collectors of bottle caps and chandeliers and lovers. Caroline at the cottage, finding the book on the bedside table, her eyes meeting Kate's, the endless recognition within them. Ava, her phone calls like beach rocks held out in the palm of a hand with the understanding that they are never the ocean itself.

She had been a river, Kate thought, the thing that took them close to death, made them suddenly, courageously, honest.

Kate looked out at the water in front of her. I know you, she said. She walked back up to the tent, where she quietly pulled her sleeping bag outside and then lay down, looking up at the stars.

Twelve days on the river, and the world was made out of small things — the distant clatter of the pots at the cook table in the morning, the scent of brewing coffee, as Kate walked barefoot across the soft sand, a metal mug in her hand. A wet bandana, drenched in the freezing river, tied around her neck on a hot afternoon, the cold water sliding down the length of her spine. The sound of the last dry bag hitting the sand as they unloaded the boats for the day. The smell of portobello mushrooms grilling, a chocolate cake baking in a Dutch oven, the cool, tart taste of a margarita made with the last of the ice they carried. The sight of a bat, conducting the night air with its wings.

The last full day of the trip. Kate lay on the rounded edge of Patty's oar boat, feeling the sun on her face, her bare arms and legs. Soon it would become too strong, she knew that by now, but for the moment, with the water lazy underneath her and the cliffs changing like an endless slide show in front of her, she was perfectly content. She looked over at her daughter, lying on the other edge almost asleep.

"Hey, Robin," she said.

"Yeah?"

"Thank you."

Robin smiled, her eyes still closed.

"While we're confessing," Robin said after a moment, "I've got something to tell you."

330

Kate raised her head and looked more closely at her daughter. Above them, on the metal cooler, Patty pretended to watch the water.

"It's not a big thing," Robin said, "it's just that I didn't want to tell you until I knew what I was thinking."

"Sure."

"I mean, I knew you and Caroline would get all excited, and I didn't want that to happen if things weren't going to work out. But I've been thinking a lot on this trip, and it seems right."

"What are we talking about?"

"Brad."

"Really?" Kate did her best to hold the eagerness out of her voice. Brad and Robin were a project that she and Caroline had first talked about when the two children were in preschool together, but had given up on long ago.

"Yeah, well — I mean, I hadn't really seen him in years. But when his dad left his mom, he called. He wanted to know what it was like for me."

Kate nodded. How grown-up her daughter sounded, how grown-up they had made her be.

"Anyway, we started talking, and then he came to visit me and . . ."

"And?"

"Mom, really. You don't want details, do you?"

"No," Kate lied. Up above her, Patty grinned.

When they rounded the next corner, they could see that two of the oar boats had pulled over next to a huge rock some thirty feet tall. Some of the younger men and women were already climbing up a path that led around the back of the rock. Kate saw Patty grimace slightly and pull into the eddy above the rock.

"What's that?" Robin asked.

"It's a jump-off rock," Patty responded. "Last big chance of the trip."

Watching Patty's expression, Kate thought not for the first time about the responsibility the guides must feel to keep their passengers in the boats and out of the fifty-degree water, protected from the heat and sun, away from rattlesnakes and falling rocks. Their group had been fairly well-behaved, but they had passed a cadre of kayakers who had showed a blissful denial of mortality. Who would pick up their bodies? Kate had wondered when she saw them aiming, one after another, for a hole in Hance rapid.

"It looks like fun," Robin said quickly, eyes alight. She jumped from the boat and joined the line heading up the path before Kate could say anything.

Patty relaxed, stretching her back, watching as the first young man took a running start and launched himself off the rock.

"You know," she said reflectively, "I sure hope none of the girls have their periods."

"Why?"

"Well, that's a lot of force when you hit the water. I did it once wearing a tampon. Had to get the darn thing pulled out of me in the emergency room."

Kate stared at her.

"You're kidding."

"Nope."

Kate looked at the young women now on the top of the rock and felt a deep, maternal urge in direct conflict with a sudden embarrassment. She may have given up showers and she no longer thought twice about walking around camp in her pajamas, but she was still not ready to yell inquiries about feminine hygiene products at the top of her lungs. She saw Robin looking down at her and signaled for her to wait. Then she scrambled out of the boat and started running up the path.

■ ■ ■ ■

None of the girls was having her period, which was a blessing, Kate thought, as one of them had jumped, screaming, just as Kate reached the top of the rock.

"It's pretty cool up here, isn't it?" Robin asked.

Kate stepped to the edge of the rock and looked down toward the river.

On one of the hikes, the group had climbed up thousands of feet above the river. Kate had looked down to see their yellow and orange rafts, small as fallen leaves on the sand below. But somehow this was different, the height at the top of the rock feeling taller with the knowledge that it was only a resting place before a larger and more spectacular commitment to the water below. Some of the group who had raced up the trail so confidently now looked more subdued at the prospect before them.

"Are you going to jump?" one of the girls asked Kate. "That would be so cool. My mom would never do that."

"Mom," Robin said quickly. "Don't do it for me. If you're going to do it, do it for you."

The tone of her daughter's voice caught

at Kate's memory. It was funny how much Robin could sound like her father at times, Kate thought.

After Robin had been born, Rick had become increasingly irritated over what he called Kate's refusal to be selfish. His leaving had changed many things, but not that — in fact, being a single parent seemed only to compound the issue. Even when the oncology doctor had given Kate the diagnosis, when her friends had urged her to claim selfishness as the only real silver lining of her illness, she had smiled and nodded and done nothing, so used to standing back that the prospect of stepping forward into a world of wants and desires seemed more exhausting than chemotherapy. It was Marion who had insisted that Kate not go by herself to her chemo appointments; it was Caroline who had literally kidnapped her for a sunny day floating across Green Lake in a rowboat.

Kate looked out at the canyon around her, at the walls that were starting to widen again, lazy and sun-filled, at the river flowing beneath her. Tonight was their last night. The last chance to stand around the prep table and try to convince Patty to put less red pepper flakes in the marinade, to smell the Dutch oven cakes that Troy turned out every evening with Martha Stewart pride. The last chance to open her eyes in the morning and watch the canyon walls wake up around her. Tomorrow they would pack up the dry bags one last time, load the rafts in the dark and float through the sunrise to the take-out spot.

It was funny how things kept coming around. On the night Rick had left for good, he asked her, frustration racing across his face, to tell him one thing she had done for herself, to tell him the last time she had ever done anything she wasn't supposed to do. Now, standing at the top of the cliff, she thought, Well I didn't die. And then, in a sudden moment of clarity, she realized how true that was, how utterly, blissfully, selfishly true.

Kate leaned over, kissed Robin's cheek and leaped off the rock, a howl of joy flying into the air.

ACKNOWLEDGMENTS

There were so many things to learn about while writing this book. Barbara Dunshee graciously gave me access to her pottery class. Pan D'Amore bakery in Port Townsend allowed me to come in during the early hours of the morning and spend the rest of the day with the smell of fresh bread lingering on my skin. Jerilynn Brousseau gave me hands-on lessons in the art of bread dough and generosity. Nancy and Bob Forten of Sweet Life Farms on Bainbridge Island handed me a warm loaf and a jar of one-hundred-year-old sourdough starter. Kim Ricketts and Michael Hebb of Onepot.org introduced me to the magic of underground restaurants. Katie Mesmer kept my feet moving for every one of those sixty miles on the 3-Day Breast Cancer Walk. Jeff McLean's travel photos were an inspiration, and Dian Campbell's knowledge of gardening was indispensable. Lucy Buckley and my sweet husband, Ben, coerced me into going down the Grand Canyon, and the guides of Canyon Explorations taught us all about grace under pressure.

Sometimes another person's words are the best. Few authors could capture the feeling of midlife better than Anne Morrow Lindbergh, whose lines from a *Gift from the Sea* are quoted in Caroline's story. I heard Paul Roe, owner of the BritishInk tattoo parlor, remark that "irreversible decisions are good for the soul" during an NPR interview, and I loved the concept so much that I borrowed his words for Marion's story.

Every word of this book has been lovingly tended by an incredible group of friends and cohorts who read my early drafts, and later drafts, and still later drafts — Gloria Attoun Bauermeister, Marjorie Osterhout, Mark Craemer, Genevieve Hagen, Nina and Bill Meierding, Holly Smith, Caitlin Bauermeister and Dorothy Rechtin. Thank you for your clear eyes and suggestions. And a deep bow of gratitude to Amy Berkower, Maja Niklovich and Rachel Kahan, whose insights and intelligence guided the manuscript into safe harbor.

And then there are those whose emotional support makes it all possible. So here's a hats-off to the camaraderie of the

Seattle7Writers, whose talent and friendship inspire me on a daily basis. And my family — Ben, Caitlin and Rylan — who opened their arms and invited these characters into their lives.

ABOUT THE AUTHOR

Erica Bauermeister is the author of the novel *The School of Essential Ingredients* and the coauthor of *500 Great Books by Women: A Reader's Guide* and *Let's Hear It for the Girls: 375 Great Books for Readers 2–14.* She lives in Seattle with her husband and their two children. She may or may not have a tattoo.